Recipes From The Dump

Recipes From The Dump

ABIGAIL STONE

AVON BOOKS NEW YORK

This is a work of fiction. None of the characters are meant to connote any living person.

The recipes in this book have not been tested by the publisher.

AVON BOOKS
A division of
The Hearst Corporation
1350 Avenue of the Americas
New York, New York 10019

Cover illustration by Marc Mongeau
Inside cover author photo by Allen Israel
Published by arrangement with W. W. Norton & Company, Inc.
Library of Congress Catalog Card Number: 95-6686
ISBN: 0-380-72882-6

First Avon Books Trade Printing: November 1996

Printed in the U.S.A.

OPM 10 9 8 7 6 5 4 3 2 1

For my mother whose unwavering
belief in me sustains me still

For Hillery, Walter, and Bianca Stone

Vorrei anche ringraziare Sandra Gilbert, essendosi
fidata delle mie capacita' da scrittrice.

Recipes

¤¤

The breaking of so great a thing should
make a greater crack.

—William Shakespeare,
Anthony and Cleopatra

Recipes From The Dump

"Hello?"

"Gabby Fulbriten?"

"Yes."

"Gabby, this is Warner, Stock and Lowe, calling in regard to your delinquent account with Fibs Plumbing. Now, we have tried in the past setting up a payment plan with you but it didn't seem to adhere. And at this point in standing, you are three hundred and . . ." I hang up. Not because I am avoiding them, but because I just looked out the window by the telephone and I saw a moose. It must be the one my neighbor Hester said was holding up traffic on route 6 just across the field. It crosses my mind to get my camera and go out to film it, but I don't. I don't even call Hester to tell her. I want nature to go on like it should . . . with the moose going along the fence near my house and nobody noticing.

WANTED TO RENT . . . LARGE SUNNY MAN WITH VIEW OF THE INTERIOR. WARM, COZY, SNUG. PETS AND KIDS OK. COMPLETE WITH ALL APPLIANCES. AVAILABLE IMMEDIATELY.

It's Saturday, and because I live out by the old stump dump, pickup trucks full of sawn-down trees and cute guys have been rolling by all morning. They clean up their yards and then they bring all the mulchable stuff out to the old stump dump at the end of this quiet road. I'm the last house by the dump, so they all have to turn around by my kitchen window. It would be comforting to see all those men happily doing Saturday yard work if only *one* of them was *my* man. Oh, well. I have three kids. Plus I listen to Shakespeare on cassette, hearing throughout the day a lot of romance and intrigue. What need I of fifty knights who probably wouldn't doff their names for me anyway?

I got a call last night from Iggy Stains out in Utah and he pretty much asked me to marry him. He's in the service, which is kind of appealing, and he is very religious, which is somehow almost electrifying, but I continue to turn him down.

It's wild country out here by the dump. Wild animals, wild storms, wild flowers. There are woodchucks in my yard and we think an otter slips up from the river below once in a while. Also, a lot of town guys come out here and drink beer and stare at my house. They stare at my house because it's the only thing to look at around here other than fields and the cows. Plus I'm usually peering out from behind the kitchen curtains, looking at their souped-up cars and feeling sort of afraid. Still, things happen out here.

I have quite a few neighbors. They are interested in me and so some days are more cluttered with visiting neighbors than others, but they tell me they mind their own business.

"We never say much to them and they don't bother with us either," says my neighbor on the other side of the road. "Tell you the truth, that's the way I enjoy it."

When she comes over she keeps her hands shoved deep into the pockets of her jeans and she talks to me sideways, in a shy manner. She baby-sits for her grandchildren too. You see a lot of that these days. The woman I bought the house from left to be closer to her grandchildren. She moved right in with her daughter-in-law. It's that way because the mothers work and the fathers are dead or gone or at work and so grandmothers come into play again. Grandmothers were an important member of the Eskimos too.

Hester liked me right away because the first thing I did when I bought the place was give her husband the freezer on the porch. It was full of horrible packages and larded-up things wedged into its corners . . . I had no use for such a huge place to store food. We live on tofu here and pizzas and homemade Amish bread now. I say "now" because my neighbor across the road, June, came down one day with a Cool Whip bowl . . . it was full of a silky yellow substance and had a recipe attached to the top. The object was to stir this for ten days until it swelled and multiplied. Then divide it into four parts, give three away to friends and make the fourth into a quick bread by adding a list of ingredients. The silky substance was dubbed "the mother."

Amish Parent for Amish Friendship Bread¤ ¤ ¤ ¤
(sometimes called "the starter")

2/3 cup sugar
2/3 cup flour
2/3 cup milk

Mix ingredients in large plastic airtight container with a lid. *Do not refrigerate.* Stir mother every day for 17 days. Follow instructions for Amish Friendship Bread.

A few notes: Be sure to open lid and stir every day or it will blow up all over the place. Be sure to use wooden spoons and glass or plastic bowls. Realize that for the next 27 days of your life the "mother" will be doubling in bulk somewhere in your home.

I made the bread, that was no problem, but when it came to giving away the mothers, I had no friends who would take them. My own mother said if I would stir it she would take it away to make the bread, but she never did. That mother died in the cupboard after bubbling for twenty-some days. Other mothers I dutifully made into the Amish bread, putting them into fluted pans and adding everything I could think of to make them sweet. Some mothers I threw in the garbage. But the more I tried to save them and feed them to someone, the more mothers there were . . . they were everywhere in my life, and when they puffed up in bowls, they'd pour over the sides and gum up everything around them. Anyway, this makes a very good loaf and I insert the recipe for you to try.

Amish Friendship Bread
(Do not use metal bowl or metal spoons)
You get the starter, called the "mother," from a friend.

Day 1: put mother in a large bowl
Day 2: stir down. Keep on broad shelf, do not refrigerate
Day 3: stir
Day 4: stir
Day 5: stir. Add 1 cup each sugar, flour, milk
Day 6: stir
Day 7: stir
Day 8: stir
Day 9: stir
Day 10: stir. Add 1 cup each sugar, flour, milk

Now you measure out 1 cup each for three people. To the remainder, add:

2/3 cup oil
3 eggs, beaten
1/2 teaspoon salt
2 teaspoons cinnamon
2 cups flour
1 1/2 teaspoons baking powder
1 cup sugar
1/2 teaspoon vanilla
1/2 teaspoon baking soda
Also, any of the following can be added:
1 cup nuts
1 cup raisins
1 cup peaches
1 cup applesauce
1 cup dates
1 cup candied fruit
1 cup pineapple, crushed
2 bananas, mashed

Makes 2 large loaves. Preheat oven to 350°. Bake 45 to 50 minutes in 2 greased and sugared loaf pans. You will find my addition of chocolate chips (indicating a longing) puts into the batter a bittersweet tang that lingers.

I first met Hester the day I had the land surveyed to buy . . . Her husband came over and introduced himself. "My wife and I live just over yonder," he said, pointing to the woods. "If you're planning on buying this land you ought to know we own your yard . . ."

"Your lawyer and I will work this out," the surveyor said, stepping up. He had a ball of twine with him. Hester's husband looked at him and turned back to me.

"My wife owns it actually. I was away during the war when she bought all this area . . . She needed a place to house herself and the kids and this suited her . . ."

"I'll handle this," the surveyor said to me.

"That's okay," I said. "I can talk to my neighbors . . ." I followed Hester's husband then, down the road, and I met Hester. She was in her kitchen with an apron on, making a summer salad when we walked in. "Mother," her husband said, sitting down at the oilcloth table, "this is our new neighbor . . . what was your name?"

"Gabby Fulbriten," I said.

"Hmmm," Hester said. She just stood there with her apron slightly wet in front, holding a tomato.

"She wants to buy your yard down there by the old Watts place."

"Hmmm," Hester said again. She turned and put her tomato in the sink. "No sense in buying it," she said, washing the tomato. "You can go ahead and use it all you want." Well, we all sort of knew this wouldn't do.

"I sort of need to own it . . . so I can make a garden . . . and so it's on my deed . . . I really want to buy that house . . . and I can't if I don't own the yard it's in . . . so . . . I would be willing to buy it from you."

"We've had more arguments over that yard," Hester began, wiping her hands on her apron. "Because I own it and the Watts think they own it, but it's on the town's record . . . I own it." Hester sat down. She looked at me and added, "Why don't your husband come down and talk with us about it?" She watched me carefully for my answer. I thought I was ruined but I told her anyway.

"I'm not married anymore," I said. "I'm raising my three kids alone."

Hester has a big heart. She sold me the land and she gave me a housewarming present . . . three dish rags crocheted by her. And she told me she was very glad I'd bought the old Watts place. I haven't seen her be forceful again since that day I met her. But her husband maintains she is always tough when it comes to protecting her children or her land.

Hester's house is full of food. They have five freezers, another neighbor informs me, and two refrigerators in the kitchen I know of . . . and quite the larder in the back. Hester herself is a quilt maker and afghan knitter. She shows me her handiwork, which is given away to the children and grandchildren. It lacks a color sense but is otherwise charming.

"Don't think for a minute they needed that freezer you gave them because I know for a fact they already have four—or maybe it's five. But they didn't need that one. . . . Course, if you didn't want it, it might just as well be in use," my neighbor June says. "Franklin probably could have found a use for it, but I said to him, 'Franklin, we don't have to have that freezer . . . She's got a right to give it to whomever she wants, poor girl.' "

I nod at this point, feeling guilty. How was I to know an old freezer would turn out to be so valuable in the neighborhood?

"I have about six pounds of butter a neighbor from my old house gave me," I tell her. "Would you want it? We don't eat butter." We move toward the pantry.

"Franklin loves butter," June tells me. "I can't eat it because of my cholesterol, but Franklin will."

We move past the shelves of rice cakes and bowls of steaming, anxious mothers, covered by cloth like middle eastern women cover their faces. June stares into the small freezer compartment shyly as I pull out the butter.

"I don't know how good it is," I say, patting the product.

"Looks okay to me . . . but like I say, Franklin loves butter. Butter, ice cream, gravy . . . sometimes I wish I'd never had my cholesterol checked."

I agree. It's a bummer.

I go out along the quiet dirt road that leads to the river and pick daisies and vetch and buttercups and twine them together into huge bouquets that sit for days all over the house until each petal has dropped and all the stems have drooped and the water is brown. My neighbors offer to show me how to plant real roses . . . where I might find a good peony bush at Agway. They offer to mow down the daisies along my fence. Hester calls her peonies "pee-*own*-ees" and rarely remembers the names of the plants she brings me. "Oh, how pretty," I say, and she says, "Hey, yeah," and I ask, "What *is* it?" and she says, "Huh? Ohhh, now I can't remember . . . somethin' . . . begins with an 'a' I think. I don't know. I'd have to look it up in my book. Anyway, where do you want it?" She helps me weed and dig out the spot and we pat the dirt around the planted item in unison. And then she talks about the new condos that are going up beside the other condos . . . the sound of the trucks all day and the dust that flies into her kitchen.

"Why don't you stop down later?" she says. "I've got a new loaf of Amish bread usin' bananas instead of applesauce. You need a starter?" She is referring to the mother recipe.

"Gee, I'm trying to get rid of three," I say.

"I froze one," she tells me, picking at the dirt on her hands from planting. "It don't bubble no more now . . . I think it died." We find this hysterically funny.

"Anyways, I better go 'fore they think somethin's happened to me."

I go back into my place, cool in the hot day, and listen to the refrigerator hum. I plan on watering the cucumbers someone gave me because the clay all around them is cracked and gray, but one thing leads to another and I haven't gotten around to it.

Last night a garbage collector stopped by to say hello. This is because I waved when he came earlier to collect. He stepped into my chaotic world of dirty dishes and cat litter and clothes piled on the washer. I'm a terrible housekeeper, other than wallpapering, and that doesn't count, I don't think. The garbage collector is named Rolando Skitchetti. He can't speak Italian, but he has a way about him . . . at least at first he had a way about him, until I found out his sister is the woman who slapped her child in a parking lot and I tried to stop her and she took a swing at me, swearing and screaming, and I said to Rolando, "I don't like your sister," and he said, "Well, maybe you don't like me either," and at that moment I thought he would hit me, but then he smiled and I smiled and I just wanted him to leave.

A neighbor of mine, Mr. Choles, comes by on his little motorized toy tractor. He's only in his sixties but he has emphysema, so he wheezes and puffs and has a hard time of it. He comes by and brings an enormous machine that slices my wood for my cookstove. I give him a loaf of Amish bread made with walnuts and chocolate chips.

"You eat a lot of chocolate, do you?" he asks, starting up the tractor mower again. "They used to give us that during the war . . ."

I want to give you an idea of what it's like out here. The woods are full of otter from the lower creek and rabbits that come out on the grass and look cheerily around. And there are sparrows and purple finches and strange exotic birds . . . there used to be a pileated woodpecker that tapped away at my willow tree but he died. I think he died . . . after a big hunting day I never saw him again. I live on the edge of a park and the locals often hunt out here . . . although since Mr. Boots brought his heifers and bulls into the lower pasture we don't have the hunting we used to. They don't like the cow pies. And I don't blame them. I quit walking in the fields and the woods when the cows came. First, they're always pooping. And then they got big and charged the kids when they took a picnic out there.

The reason I'm telling you this is because I want you to become familiar with the landmarks, the surroundings. I want it to be as comfy as watching TV for you to read this book. I want you to lean back into a La-Z-Boy recliner or a wrap-around couch and see the world of Leadbelly, Vermont, just as if you were living in it. Mr. Boots, for example, is the cowman. When he arrives in his red car (belongs to his wife,

Dorothy Stella Boots) he gets out and sits on the fence awhile, calls his cows maybe, they look up from far away, and then in a straggling group move toward him, slowly, and then faster and faster . . . rushing at the end, colliding into each other to get to Mr. Boots first. He goes over the fence and stands in amongst them, and lets them shove him around a little, shouts at them occasionally, "Hey, Jack, cut it out! Cut it out! *Hey!*" But they don't cut it out. Sometimes while I watch I bite my cheek all out of shape and consider calling the fire station to come help him . . . they seem so insistent to get him down. They push and push . . . and he won't get out of there. He just gets corralled around the field, shouting.

Living near the dump, it's peaceful mostly. The land beyond my house slopes down pretty quick into the river and the electric plant. I don't see any of that because of the sumac trees, but I can hear the ducks early in the morning down on the river, and the honking that goes on down there is tremendous.

The people who used to own my house killed everything they could lay their hands on: ducks, hogs, chickens, cows, hens, their own dog. The old lady (the mother of the whole brood that sold me the place) lived here till her husband died. There are hooks all over the property where he hung meat to drip and dry. They had silver freezers in the yard to smoke things, and the house stank of pickled animals.

"Best man a woman could have," she confided in

me as I moved in. She had brought a picnic to the yard and was eating on the grass on a blanket while I carried boxes.

"Nobody coulda had nothin' compared to him." She panted after she spoke and then took a bite of her sandwich. "Yup. He spoiled me," she said.

I've been husband hunting. I have. And there is nobody out there, I promise. At least not for a woman in her thirties, like me, for instance. But then maybe we are all allowed a certain number of husbands, much like how we are born with a set amount of fertile eggs, and once those have been used up, that's it. No more. And since I have had two husbands (not actually *husbands* in the legal sense, but . . . close enough) . . . since I've had these two . . . maybe that's it for me. But I can't accept that.

This Rolando Skitchetti has a lunatic sister and he says "Yeah, they fired me" over everything I bring up.

"Boy, the Grand Union has a special on this week on candy and we got . . ."

"Yeah, they fired me," he responds gloomily.

"Where else have you worked?"

"I'm good at truck driving and that's it. Used to drive bread trucks but yeah, they fired me. I got a chip on my shoulder one day and they fired me."

I don't know . . . I'm about five feet four inches tall; I weigh more than I should; I have long brown hair;

brown eyes; and large useful hands. I enjoy a variety of things. So why is it impossible to meet any men? Incidentally, where *are* the men?

And so the husband hunt continues. I read somewhere that of all the divorced baby boomers, the kids rarely see their fathers. So I hunt for a new one.

A few prospects. One guy would really like to be my husband, but he already has five kids, so with mine we would have eight, and I'm not sure he loves me for me or for my mothering techniques. He is slightly overweight, but that's okay; I am too. And he has lost most of his hair. In fact, one Halloween he showed me his toupee, and I was somewhat embarrassed. He seems to drink a lot of beer and then gets amorous, which I could still live with except that he says pretty peculiar things like " 'Domination' is the key word." I don't know what he meant; it just made me feel strange is all. No, he won't do.

Probably one of the main reasons I haven't remarried is the fact that I'm a messy housekeeper. Now I know this is a dumb reason, but a lot of men find tripping over garbage bags full of dirty laundry unsavory. I don't know, I think unsavory would be a toupee, but men are different from women, and I've seen their faces when they stumble and pitch forward onto the bags of laundry or the Cheerios that have spilled all over the floor. I don't get around to washing the dishes much either, so maybe the rotting cantaloupe and spaghetti in the sink turns them off. Me, I lose passion over hair slipping off the head and into my caressing hands . . . you know . . . toupee-type hair.

This morning the cat drank nearly all the fish water and was lapping the edges of the fish bowl like a connoisseur at an elegant restaurant . . . inching deliciously down the bowl toward the paté. The goldfish swam in a nervous circle, lower and lower. Of course I saved it. That's why I'm here, isn't it?

The garbage collector, Rolando Skitchetti, insisted on coming over. When he arrived, he grabbed me as though he had been thinking about me too much. He had on an old V-neck sweater, and his chest hair poked through the weave. He sat in a gloomy hump on one of my antique chairs and talked for half an hour.

"You let me know if I'm runnin' my mouth too much," he said, between topics. "People say I run my mouth and I guess I do. I guess I'm just inquisitive, that's all . . . I don't know. Some people don't care to find out the answer but I'm not that way. Me, I like to know. My sister's gettin' married next weekend—jeez, I didn't even know she was in love. We never used to like each other, growin' up. Now when I call she says, 'Ohhh, Rolando! Hoi! Hoi! What's happening?' Never used to get along. But that's okay . . . I'm easygoin'. Yup. Boy, I like to look at your face. Guess you make me feel like a kid again. I don't know why. I used to play bass. Yup. Even had groupies."

Rolando told me he was changing jobs, would no longer be picking up my garbage. Planned on settling down soon. I told him I was sick and that he had to go home.

I would like to hear from other women who are on a similar quest. Do they run into little problems like I do? Is it my locale, or perhaps my approach? Is the shortage a reality? You hear about it . . . One in fifteen women find a second husband . . . Joan Collins is more apt to land on the moon than a divorced woman is to find a second husband. Things like this bog one down. You know, if they made you feel more *upbeat* about it maybe you could smile once in a while and meet a guy. But the odds are against you and the stats are against you and the press is against you, so where are you? Alone at the fitness club wondering why you are getting forever into shape just to sleep alone in your size eight silk pajamas.

Morning happens quietly, with birds singing. The robins are back from the Bahamas and the starlings roost in hordes on the dead trees across the road. The dog pees at 6:30 A.M. on the wide pine kitchen floor, a tradition with her since old age. The cat looks for the litter box, gives up too soon. Morning—a secretive thing that draws you from your bed to make tea and ponder. And to get the children ready for school so they won't miss the bus.

❧

On any particular day you will find the house a mess, the children asleep, and me in charge, pulling clothes from drawers, attempting to dress the army. The army doesn't want to get out of bed. They lie there, big hamsters, furless but appealing, and they allow me to put their arms into small sleeves and to shove their skinny warm legs into pants legs. My oldest daughter, Shelley, gets up at the crack of dawn and dresses herself to the beat of Bette Midler. Shelley is small-boned and delicate, with very large, very sad, brown eyes. Her father, Gerry, is tall (he still keeps in touch), but Shelley remains short because, I think, of the Neomul-soy she lived on as an infant. She couldn't tolerate milk so we had to find this soy formula for her and personally, I think it made her short.

❧

Last night I had a dream about Muslim men. One of them was in love with me. They brought me to meet their family but the mother disapproved. I realized my feet were bare and dirty and the family was dressed in jeweled clothes. That's a variation on the grubby nightgown theme. Usually I dream that I am wearing a grubby nightgown and the man I love is in a suit and another woman is there in a beautiful dress and I am mortified. King Richard was mortified too, when they stripped him of his crown. I insert a sorrowful recipe. A soup to cry in.

King Richard the Second Soup ¤¤¤¤¤¤¤¤¤¤¤¤¤

1. *4 whole onions, because he suffered wholly the desertion of his subjects; like layers of an onion, they slipped away from him*
2. *2 carrots, as the carrot dangled before his nose, an offering if he would abdicate civilly to Edward*
3. *4 cups sorrel leaves—like sorrow, the soup should be bitter with it*
4. *2 cups dandelion greens, to signify his young queen, who in her death drove the young king to the brink. No reason for her death . . . the greens should be slightly wilted.*
5. *1 meat bone, to represent Edward, whose children were damned by Richard to pay for usurping the throne. If the meat bone is ham, it shows his pigginess and greed to wrench from his king that rightful crown. If the meat bone is beef, let it represent stupidity, pushiness, brawn, and barrenlessness.*
6. *Salt to taste, for they took his crown* and *wanted him to admit his guilt (he would not)*
7. *Water, all things must pass.*

Hester took a walk with me recently, and we walked to the river's edge where the water rushes over the cement dam and gives the town electricity. She hurried forward, telling me, "This is where the boys used ta fish. You could walk right t'over there and cross the river . . ." pointing to the opposite bank. She looked gloomy. She has a lump in her breast that they tell her must be removed.

"Hey-yup. The kids had picnics here. Now I walk here every day in the summer. They built that dam up all new, and see here? It's cracked already."

We stepped across a wooden crossway and came up the other edge, doubling back through the electric plant. Hester wrapped her winter jacket closer around her chest. She looked very sad, and I figured it was her breast that was bothering her. They had put her through stress tests to see if she could survive an operation, and they thought she would. Anyway, we ended up near my house and I didn't want her to come in on account of the place was a wreck. She's always telling me how somebody or other has a dirty house, and I didn't want her to see mine in that state.

"You a good swimmer?" Hester asked me, approaching my front door.

"Sort of," I said. "I can keep above water. I'm not that good, but yeah. Why? Do you wanna go swimming?"

"No. I don't swim," she said. We were in front of my kitchen door now, so I opened the door and we went in, the shock of the mess even sweeping me away for a minute. "God, I never get a chance to get anything done . . ." I offered.

"Not since that time I almost drownd-ed," she said.

"Oh?"

"When we was kids we used to go out to this place in a meadow that was pretty well, sandy, you know, and we'd swim there . . . There was a branch hung out over the water . . . We were all sitting on that branch, dangling our feet, when the branch broke and in we went." Hester sort of smiled.

"My brother had to drag me up by my hair . . . prit near was drownd-ed." She looked around the kitchen then, and then at me.

"You don't swim neither?"

"No," I said. "My mother was afraid we'd be killed if we went in the water. She let me go in some, but not enough to learn how to swim."

I began wiping off the kitchen table. Watermelon rinds were withering here and there, and the sweet juice had hardened on the wood floor.

"Well, I better get back. They'll think I fell in the crick," she said. I showed her the sampler quilt I was starting to work on. She said she'd teach me how to embroider later on, if I still wanted to when the sampler was done.

"I want to embroider flowers around on it," I said.

"Hey-yup," Hester said. "Maybe I'll go a little farther on my walk . . . just down to the dump. . . ." She turned and trotted out of my dooryard (that's what she calls the area around the front door) and went off in the direction of the dump.

The dump is a swell place to walk because it's peaceful, but I fear the ground will give way. It's been turned over so many times . . . filled with tin cans and old stoves . . . There's a drop-off all around three sides of it too, and it borders my land. I feel I've bought a place on the precipice, like the fool in the tarot pack . . . the brink of life or death. The brink of knowledge or understanding. I have a Spanish tarot pack with El Loco as the fool. But Hester has lived out here for thirty years and she is used to the old town dump. When it opened there used to be big rats out here, but that ended in the seventies when townspeople marched against it with burning candles and got the place shut down.

Dump Cookout ¤¤¤¤¤¤¤¤¤¤¤¤¤¤¤¤¤¤¤¤¤¤¤¤¤¤¤¤

Burger rolls
Stack of paper plates
One pound of ground beef
Cokes in plastic bottles
Jumbo bags of chips

Gather the family together and cook hamburgers over charcoal briquette grill outside. Let a few paper plates fly around the yard to give it the "down home at the dump" look. Spill Coke. Give the kids each a plate and let them pour their own ketchup. Allow smears to dry on everything. Eat quickly and wander off.

Sometimes Hester "sees my kids to the bus" when I'm working early at the grocery . . . she calls it that . . . "I'll see your kids to the bus if you want," she had said once . . . so whenever I have to be at work early, Hester will give my children a call after I leave and make sure they are on the way to the bus down the road. When they pass her place she comes and sort of cheers them on. But this is only when I have to go to work early. The Hurry Up food mart usually lets me work during school hours, but once in a while I have to take someone else's shift. I hate doing it but if I don't I'm considered a spoil-sport and the scorn of the other employees isn't worth the inconvenience. I don't just check out; I also handle the books. Anyway, all the checkout females like working early because that's when the Today & Yesterday food-chain representative is often seen driving to work. He has a purple Ferrari and he's apparently very handsome . . . "a big teddy bear with curly hair" is how he's described. Actually I've always wanted to meet him but I've never even seen his vehicle. His name is Mr. Marrow and he started out as a butcher.

Hester's lump in her breast is common knowledge around the neighborhood. People talk about it like they discuss how much snow fell on the mountain or which daughter is getting married in June. Hester listens with one anxious hand across her mouth, like she's afraid of what might be said. The other night, I was at her house, exchanging scrap pieces for quilts because she's making a grab-bag type and I'm doing the Ohio star. Her sister's cousin was there from Brainwater, and she began asking after Hester's lump.

"You hear when they want you in for?" she asked. I was drinking tea Hester had made me and eating one of Hester's homemade cookies.

"Doctor wants me in sometime next week . . . to let me know . . . when I go in."

"Same thing happened to my first husband, Hester," she went on. She had strange hypnotic glasses on and yet I saw her eyes tearing through the lenses. "They removed a *five-pounder* from him. Why, they had to pull ribs, remove organs . . . just to get that five-pound tumor out."

I said "wow" at that point, wasn't medicine amazing? and the cousin said, "Course he died anyway," and Hester's face was covered with her anxious hand. "He only lived three months," the cousin said, and her eyes reddened. "Now Tommy has to go in for prostate. And if that goes, why then they'll want at that hernia too. His doctor checked the right side and there was nothing . . . and then the left, and he said 'Uh-oh! Better come in next week.' So he will."

Hester said nothing. "They've learned a lot in the last few years," I offered, letting my cookie lie quietly next to my tea. Always on a diet. Never losing weight. That's me all over. I weigh more now than I did when . . . oh, well, why paint a bad picture?

Hester's cousin, it turns out, is the wife of the man who has a brother who teaches my kids piano. This area is very connected.

"Hey-yup," she said, brushing crumbs away, "her husband has a brother teaches your kids. He told me." Hester bends forward when she laughs, hugging her wounded chest. And we all have more tea and quit resisting the cookies. After all, it's a dull Sunday, and who's going to see me anyhow? The men in the condominiums are all married and the local town guys are . . . well . . .

"I wish they could put it off though," I said, referring to the operation.

"Well, they *can't,"* Hester said. "They gotta get it before it turns." I wondered about this remark as I walked home. Turns where? Turns around? Is it free-floating? Will it punch out, say, of her eye or something? Is it a five-pounder? I worry about Hester because she is so real to me. She is the only woman I know who makes all her own blankets and cans all her own winter food, even cans some for her grown children and their families, though her kids all have homes and jobs scattered around throughout the county. On holidays, her kids and their families come to Hester's house for dinner. Sometimes I walk past when they are there, the road is lined up with their cars and I can see the grandchildren sitting in the living room . . . I can see the windows steamed up with so many people talking and breathing in there at once. And Hester makes all her meals from scratch, and bakes every cookie the grandchildren eat, and puts vegetables in the root cellar. People don't go through such labors anymore. Once, when I had cut my toe, she tried to get me to soak it in lye.

"You take and put your foot in the lysine and it'll take the swellin' down," she said, pushing a dark yellow bottle at me. I backed away, refusing.

"I'll use hydrogen peroxide," I said.

"This is what we always used when we was kids," she said. "Just put your whole foot in there and it'll take the swellin' . . . down . . ."

But I read the label and it was for toilets.

On to the mail to cheer us up! The letter that is always in the box when I am hoping for some real communication . . . "Wishing you and yours many blessings, from Elvira Dirge" (who, by the way, I can't recall . . . even to figure out where she is from). Elvira? I just can't place it. But every Friday when I yearn for the truth, for a boost of invigorating love, when I hunger for a note from an ex-lover, a longtime fan, that grocery store representative, I get Elvira junk mail . . . "Wishing yours a blessing." And, by the way, I've been reading the personals. (Well, the weather has taken a nasty turn for the worse, and the fires needed building so I read the personals before I crumpled them up. I'm sure everybody does it.) And something really killed me. I mean, it became so apparent . . . what's wrong with our culture . . . because that's always preying on my mind . . . *men* are not the hunting, dangerous, scary, Adam's apple-bulging guys they used to be. And yet people don't seem to pay attention to that . . .

> SINGLE WHITE MALE, 35, SEEKS STRONG, INDEPENDENT, SERIOUS, FUNNY WOMAN OF ANY SIZE. I AM KIND, LOVING, GENTLE, DOCILE, HARMLESS AND WARM . . . LOOKING FOR TEDDY BEAR RELATIONSHIP . . . LOTS OF HUGS. SEX NOT IMPORTANT. LET'S GET TO KNOW EACH OTHER!

Below that was a hot line for a rape crisis center, a rape survivor group, a women who feel psychologically raped group, and a rape rally forthcoming.

> DIVORCED WHITE MALE SEEKS GENTLE, UNFEARFUL RELATIONSHIP. NONSMOKER, NONDRINKER, NONMEAT EATER, WITH VASECTOMY; LOOKING FOR WALKS IN THE MOONLIGHT AND SPIRITUAL GROWTH.

It hits me, *bang,* what's going on. And yet, do I dare express myself here? Is it possible we long to return to the angry, prowling, fierce male lion who clawed his prey and licked his wife? I mean, am I the only one who is turned off by this gentle, harmless, spermless new male?

> DIVORCED SINGLE WHITE GAY MALE LOOKING (AT LAST!) FOR SERIOUS MONOGAMOUS RELATIONSHIP. I AM GENTLE, KIND, FULL OF GOOD TIMES AND FUN-LOVING. I LOOK STRAIGHT AND SEEK SAME IN PARTNER. CALL ME, LET'S TAKE A CHANCE.

> MACHO HUNK WITH BROWN HAIR AND BIG BICEPS (GREEN EYES) WANTS YOU! I GET OUT OF PRISON IN JUNE.

> RAPE CRISIS CENTER IN NEED OF MORE FUNDS! WOMEN IN CRISIS HOT LINE SEEKS MORE FEDERAL FUNDING. RAPE CENTER THRIVING IN WAHAKIS, NM.

But where are all these rapists? It's not that I think that's the right thing to ask, but all the men I meet or read about in the want ads are either meek and deflated or shrill and gay. Women have become macho toughies, and a lot of them are gay too. A lot of these gay women are friends with gay men. They all get together in the evening, but the visual effect is disturbing.

Today I bumped into a guy who has hinted at attraction toward me. These days that's the best you can hope for. I remember when guys used to drive around in cars that chugged and call out to me, "Hey, c'mere," and I'd say, "Me?" and they'd say, "You heard me, c'mere," and I'd go because it was the sheer excitement of the hunt. Now, men twist their hands while they talk to me and say, "Well, you're looking well. Have you been doing aerobics?" and they turn their heads to the side.

"I'm trying to work out some every day," they confide. "I walk my son to school and I drink weak coffee when I'm famished . . . keeps me from raiding the fridge." I am appalled.

"Do I have your number?" he continues, and I realize he's interested in me. No, he hasn't looked me up and down like in the old days, but he's implying he'd like to be phone friends. "I've never lost those ten pounds I put on after the vasectomy," he says.

SINGLE WHITE MALE IN 50S, PHYSICALLY FIT AND LEAN SEEKS FEMALE IN LATE 20S TO EARLY 40S FOR DISCUSSION OF WHAT IT ALL MEANS. I ENJOY HIKING AND CANDLELIGHT.

This seems funny. They all like candlelight.

In the morning, my six-year-old son, J.D., gets out of bed and comes into the bathroom, rubbing his eyes. I'm in there. I got up early and had a fight with my preteen daughter, Shelley. Shelley wants to cut her hair so she'll fit in better. Of course, I don't want her to cut her hair and fit in better. Her hair is so beautiful. J.D., I notice, is covered with brown goo. "Ohhh, no!" I say when I see him. He turns on the water, somnambulistlike, and shivers when it touches his fingers.

"Here . . . here, let me . . . did you poop in the bed, J.D.?" I ask him.

"No. I just rolled in it. It's throw-up."

"Ewwww! Gross!" Shelley shrieks, coming into the bathroom fascinated. As I gingerly rub him with soap, a strong smell of chocolate wafts up from his skin.

"Oh, it's chocolate. Did you eat your chocolate Easter bunny in bed last night, J.D.?" I ask.

"No," he says.

"Oh yeah, right," Shelley says, and whisks through the bathroom, in tears again over her hair. "Why can't I just have it *trimmed*?"

My younger daughter, Grace, is still in bed, savoring the two dollars she found under her pillow in place of the lost tooth. She's happy that her friend is coming over after school. When I come into the room to survey the chocolatey bed, she looks up happily at me and says, "Now I have three dollars!"

After the children have gone to school on the bus, I take a bag of garbage outside to the trash barrel by the road. Today is Earth Day, and Grace went to school in a green shirt in order that the first grade would look like little blades of grass. The trash barrel by the road will be dumped later into a bigger truck that will take it to some landfill that is probably nearly filled, and I feel guilty as I drop in my green bag. I think about how I should reuse things. I remember an old boyfriend and how he folded grocery bags and took them back to the store. I go inside to squash soup cans.

*

The birds sing hallelujah songs to each other because it is spring. The road no longer has rivulets along its edges, and the mud is drying in the field across the road. I breathe in edge-of-the-old-dump air and sigh. The robins are back. The starlings have come and gone . . . they covered the dead trees in the field for weeks, screaming and fluttering up in the air nervously and then settling again and again. . . . Hester didn't care for them and I think maybe she didn't let them eat at her feeder. One night, before dark really, when I had seen the sky black with their crowded wings, I had rushed to the store and purchased several bags of seed and flung them in a heap on a hill. The pile was there still. Not a bird had touched it. I walked carefully back to the house . . . dog poop was all over the spring yard.

*

I called my mother last night. Who would call their mother at 3:30 in the morning for no reason? But I know that if it is a dark night with an edge to it, probably she'll be awake. "Hi, honey, what's up?"

"Nothing."

"I'm just lying here reading the biography of Oscar Wilde. Apparently he was a sweet man."

"I've been sick all day," I said.

"Say, I had this wild thing happen to me . . . this student wrote me an angry four-page tirade because I panned T. S. Eliot. My God, all I said was that he lifted lines from other writers . . ."

My house was cold and the dog scratched herself endlessly in the kitchen. I could hear, from my seat on the stairs, all the night sounds. The tick of the stove expanding as the logs burned, the rattle of a window with the wind's trying to get in, the silence of my children asleep.

"Well, hell, Yeats was brilliant," my mother was saying. "So everything okay?"

"Yeah," I said. "I'm gonna hang up now."

"All right, sweetie. Okay, honey. Bye, darling. I love you. Give everybody a kiss . . ."

Maybe she would have said more, but I hung up and went to bed. My son had gotten in my bed while I was on the phone. His sweet chocolate-smelling body was draped widthwise on my bed like a rag doll. Gee, you'd think after that bath and the fresh clothes I put on him he wouldn't smell like this. But chocolate permeates.

When I was little my sister and I played in the cow pastures around our country home. When I say country I don't mean *Country Life*. I mean no water in the house, no furnace, kerosene lamps . . . I don't know whether my mother just *liked* living the brutal life or if we were forced to out of poverty. After my father died, we lived on Social Security while mother worked at various teaching jobs, cried all the time and sometimes disappeared in the old barn. Once I went in there and she was sitting on the red Victorian couch that she had bought at an auction for five dollars and she was crying. "Mommy, what are you doing in the barn?" I said, stepping over piles of boards to get to where she was perched. She looked (now that I think back) like a beautiful bird that had gotten trapped in the barn. Sometimes that happened and Mother had to finagle her way through the barn, climbing on ladders and swinging from the rafters to get the bird out of the wooden window. "I'm thinking," my mother said, her voice was brief and strange. I can't forget that because I didn't stay in the barn . . . I left . . . and later she was in the kitchen making spaghetti and garlic bread and who knows what she had been doing in there.

Without warning, Mother would put all of us in the car and pack a lot of stuff in with us, like Kleenex and cheese and rye bread and cat food and poetry books and blankets, and off we'd go to visit Grama Fulbriten in Chicago. Grama Fulbriten had blue and white hair and lived in a very fancy apartment that you could only get to by an elevator. It took us three days to get to Chicago from Vermont because we had to stop in Buffalo to spend the night at Mommy's friends' house and they always all stayed up all night and didn't get up till late afternoon the next day. These were old friends of my father's. He was a professor and they had a stone fortress-type house with a swimming pool. I loved going there because the mother was very lenient and while my mother read and laughed and talked all night, we all got to swim in their heated indoor pool and do daredevil things that my mother would have died if she'd known. That's where I got my ears pierced . . . One of their kids took ice cubes and froze my ears and then pierced them with a safety pin. After Buffalo, we were back on the highway again, driving the old red and white Ford through snowstorms on our way to visit Grama Fulbriten. My mother hated Grama Fulbriten. She had been against my mother and father's marrying and after my father died Grama sort of blamed my mother and my mother blamed Grama Fulbriten.

On the way across the country, Mommy stopped only for coffee and to let us pee. We never stayed in hotels or had dinners at restaurants like other people. We were jammed to the scuppers, as my mother always said, and we stayed that way till we got there, and one of my mother's rules was no falling asleep. This was because our car was very old and full of holes and Mother thought it might be leaking carbon monoxide poisoning and if somebody fell asleep, then she thought they were dying and we had to roll down all the windows and sing loudly so we would stay awake. I can't remember why we always crossed the country in the dead of winter but it was so cold with the windows all rolled down. "My gal's a corker, she's a New Yorker . . . I give her everything to keep her in style . . . she's got a pair of lips just like potato chips, oh boy that's where my money goes!" My mother started the song and we picked it up and sang verses for hours before my sister Nina would say, "Let's do the one with the Alice blue gown in it" and my family would sing that one. I never learned that one. It was one of their secret things . . . my older sister and my mother and Nina. With us on all the trips was our long-haired dachshund with epilepsy named Cocoa Poo Poo and our cocker spaniel named Poochie and our occasional stray that was usually pregnant and often had puppies going through Ohio, and of course the small animals . . . I had a hamster named Himmins, which rode the trip in a wastepaper basket. By the time we reached Chicago, we were tired and the dogs were all car sick. I couldn't wait to see Grama Fulbriten.

Up the elevator with the dogs on leashes and my mother already upset . . . "I'm afraid the car will get towed where it is . . ." The elevator doors slide open and we are in a hallway . . . Grama Fulbriten opens her gold door and we see her wave. "Come, come . . . oh not dogs!" Grama Fulbriten hated dogs. "Hide the hamster," Mother whispered to me. I was carrying Himmins in my coat pocket. "Hello, Mother," my mother said to my father's mother.

"Oh . . . look how lovely the children are . . . come in . . . not the dogs . . . the dogs have to stay in the car!" When we all stepped into her apartment, it was like walking into a TV show. She had white carpeting and a big fake purple stuffed poodle in the corner of her living room. She had an oil painting of Daddy on the wall in a huge gilt frame. Her bathroom was completely purple . . . even the toilet paper was purple. Even the tub was purple. I walked through her apartment thinking how wonderful it was and I could hear Grama and Mommy beginning to fight. "Oh don't be silly. You're being rude . . . we came all this way just to see you. Now don't worry about the dogs . . ."

"You didn't bring the rat, did you?" Grama asked. I could smell dinner cooking in her brand-new oven. Everything was so new. "I don't want that little animal in my home."

"If you make us leave now, we may have an accident . . . it's dark and there's a snowstorm coming . . . couldn't we just spend the night and have a nice time?" Grama Fulbriten slammed a door.

"I won't come out of here until you tell me that you

didn't bring the rat!" she screamed. "I am afraid of rodents."

"It's a hamster," Mommy said.

The woman at the end of the road adopted a baby last week. It was shipped up from the south and we're all very excited. I mean, adoption is a difficult thing to do these days. It's as hard as having a multiple birth or getting pregnant in a petrie dish, right? A lot of people get pregnant in petrie dishes these days. I have a theory on the falling fertility rate—if you would bear with me? I thank you.

Compare. In the olden days, women stayed home and had children and sat by the fire stirring and sewing . . . They did a lot of physical labor and either died or were very healthy. Now, they go out to work . . . business execs and trash incinerator supervisors. Their bodies don't view this as a childbearing body . . . and so they don't drop eggs. And men are hardly necessary anymore other than the actual *act,* you know, so their bodies have decided to shut down too. Also, the male body does not want to reproduce because it has been shunted around and ignored and replaced by all these adequate females. Now the truth is, women probably *are* superior . . . but so what? We took big jobs. We put the necessary stuff in sperm banks. We learned that doctors aren't needed much at birth. We began to double up: single mom seeks same to share Victorian house in the country, three to six kids O.K. Nonsmoker, nondrinker. We quickly began obliterating the man. Where is his place? We don't need him to hunt; we have the Grand Union. We don't need him to bring home the bacon, equal pay and women in the job force and all that rot. We don't need him to father the kids once we've had them because we discovered that fathers are unuseful. They get in the way . . . you know, they show up on Sundays to take the kids out, and the kids look uncomfortable and the father looks anxious. The father peers into the doorway like a curious outsider to see if it is homey, to see if he is missed or if he ever existed.

I'm feeling sarcastic today. I'm feverish and sweaty from the stomach flu and I'm sitting in the sun in the morning feeling hateful and sarcastic. The children are all in school and my house is a mess. What will I do? Will I stay in bed and feel sick again? Will I tackle the housecleaning? Perhaps a ride in the dangerous car, to Ames, say, where I can look at video movies and say to myself, "If I had forty dollars, I'd buy *Lonely Guy* and *The Hustler* with Paul Newman in it." Will I feel better?

Yes, what makes a man necessary? Here we are, all self-sufficient, while the men seek spiritual growth and nonsmokers, and we are terribly strong from aerobic workouts and pushups, but we're terribly lonely. Don't we want to go back?

NONSMOKING CAVE DWELLER SEEKS LONG-HAIRED WOMAN TO SLEEP WITH ON A TIGER SKIN. MUST BE ABLE TO BEAR CHILDREN AND BE PULLED AROUND A LOT.

In the grade schools and high schools, conservation and ecology rage onward in a desperate bid to save the planet. The grade school in town recently had a big Earth Day celebration where the classes sang songs about their duties. My children learned something that went like this: "I am responsible for what goes in my planet." And then they all trooped outside behind the playground and stood in a circle singing ". . . this land is your land, this land is my land . . ." My children were mostly interested in the huge beach ball that rolled in the circle, representing Earth.

"Now please remember to take your recycled products and trash bags to the front as you file back to your classes. Thank you" kept booming over a loudspeaker. I was there to pick up my son from kindergarten; otherwise, he has to ride the school bus home at noon and it takes two hours because they have to travel all over the county. After he got in the car I rolled up the windows and could no longer hear any of the celebrations going on. We drove to McDonald's and had hamburgers and put the foam boxes in the correct receptacle. Then we went home—out by the old town dump, long closed but still a monument to garbage. . . . For instance, at the entrance to the old dump a rusting doll buggy has

rested upside down since we moved here, beside part of a twisted swing set. My son went inside and turned on the TV.

"I'll have a candy bar if you want me to," he called down the stairs.

I was sitting at the table, rereading yesterday's mail from Elvira Dirge. "Many, many blessings" the letter began. There was no postmark, so probably Mrs. Dirge snuck up to my mailbox after dark to leave it . . . or maybe right in broad daylight when I wasn't home. But who's to say Elvira is religious? "Blessings" could be a figure of speech.

I guess Earth Day is a good idea . . . but what worries me is not garbage but condos. I wish they would stop erecting condos like Lego sets everywhere . . . Huge communities of condo dwellers now are spread everywhere. Just down the road from my home they've slapped up about thirty new units this winter alone. First they would dynamite for a week, making the earth tremble and creak. Sirens went off and I was afraid my place would slide off the ledge it sits on and slip into the river below us. Then they poured cement everywhere and made basements . . . or did they? Anyway, they spent a few weeks putting up drywall and laying in much foam. There were foam boards stacked up and distributed, then some men came and hammered for a day or so—actually, there was never much hammering going on at the condo site . . . I think they glued much of it. So now we have a condominium town across the field. Right now, with the fog's covering half the field outside the windows, I can't see the condo town and it feels almost like the country out here. If I blur my eyes just a bit when I look, I can skip right over the asphalt wrinkling the road and it all seems so peaceful. Birds twitter in the dead trees on the fields' edges; the fog makes it all seem surreal and clean. But I heard they are going to saw down the trees that are dead because they're planning a larger "village." More units are expected by the fall of this year. "More units are expected." It sounds like enemy troops, doesn't it? And come to think of it, Elvira Dirge might live over there . . . maybe she crosses the field with the envelope early in the morning, before going to church.

> CHURCHGOING MAN SEEKS CHURCHGOING WOMAN TO SHARE CHURCH PICNICS WITH AND CHURCH SOCIALS. MUST HAVE A STRONG SENSE OF THE GOSPEL AND MUST KNOW JESUS. I ENJOY CANDLELIGHT.

Church is comforting, actually. There is a sense of family and of secret rites when you all get together in the church. The ripping of the bread, the little disposable plastic cups of water, the kindly eyes of the church leaders—well, some of them look mighty scary—but the kindly feeling that permeates, the nods and hugs of the members who haven't seen you since last Easter, the intimacy of pew sitting.

To be truthful, I was a Mormon for two years. Technically, I still am. They call me "inactive" because I don't attend Sunday services anymore.

But what has this to do with condominiums? I digress.

Earthling Junket

1 meek and tender earthling, soaked overnight in wine
2 cups brains, washed (brainwashing is a simple procedure—check your local listings)
1/2 teaspoon diet soda
6 full measures earthling desires

Put earthling in saucer while you assemble recipe. Brainwash and boil with the diet soda over a medium flame. The secret to the success of this recipe is to vary the earthling desires each time you concoct it for your group or team. (We always assume you are in a group or on a team.) Here are some suggestions for desires:

1) to own a condo in the country
2) to purchase that second VCR for the bedroom
3) to pay off the MasterCard and the car loan!
4) to go to Hawaii, Florida, Alaska, Bermuda

5) to finish the porch, the garage, the Monopoly game
6) to put your kids through camp, ballet classes, violin lessons, college

Add at least 6 desires at the same time as you dump saucer with earthling into the shallow pan. Let swim around until spoon will stand in the thickness. Pour into dessert dishes and refrigerate until your class or organization arrives in casual wear. Blend in and serve.

Hester went to the hospital today to get operated on. I didn't ask the details and she doesn't volunteer much, but she did tell me her doctor was very nice to her and spent a lot of time telling her the risks. She said he was very kind. So Hester is gone. She took her suitcase, toothbrush and trappings all away to the hospital. I hugged her good-bye. Maybe I'll never see her again. She's getting old and it's a dangerous operation . . . her husband is afraid to go to the hospital at all. He's claustrophobic. But she'll be all right alone. I mean, we all have to meet God alone anyway. (That's the Mormon in me hollering to get out.) Last night Hester and I took a walk down by the raging river; raging because spring is here and what snow we had this winter melted and went into the river. And the water roils brown and frothy and calls to us to fling ourselves in and not to fear the hospital anymore. Hester looks frightened. I say, "Boy, you'll be so happy when you've got all this behind you."

And she says, "Hey, yeah. But I didn't get the yard raked," and we fall silent. Does this mean she will never get the chance to rake again? I can't say anything . . . she has already decided and there's no stopping it now. The doctors are waiting to cut her open. They have polished the instruments and are waiting for her. Having told her of the risks, they are eager to start . . . call for the scalpel and adjust the face masks. She has to go now. So she went, and there is an appalling silence on the street, like there is no one left. It's just the birds, the sad black birds around her feeder, the children in my yard, splashing in the cold spring puddles, and me, wondering if she died under the anesthesia. And me also wondering what the mailman is going to bring me.

LOOKING FOR LOVE? WRITE TO P.W. #24 AND SEND PHOTO FOR QUICK RESPONSE! I LOVE QUIET WALKS, GOOD FOOD, NONSMOKER, CANDLELIGHT AND SLIM YOU. YES, YOU. YOU WEIGH 120 OR LESS, YOU LOVE CANDLELIGHT AND YOU THINK THERE MIGHT BE MORE TO THE SKY THAN THE CONSTELLATIONS. YOU'RE A NONSMOKER, NONDRINKER, NO KIDS, AND YOU'RE FUN-LOVING! I'M SICK OF LOOKING FOR YOU! WRITE SOON.

Sometimes I feel like we'll never get together again. I mean men and women. Here we are, stuck dreaming about each other but too afraid to say anything other than candlelight.

I dreamed about the food-chain representative, and in this dream I heard his voice, harmless and kind, asking me strange things. "Was that résumé I sent him all autobiographical?" "Did I watch television?" I was lulled into a conversation with him, his silky voice so beautiful and rhythmical. Suddenly it became harsh and controlling. Later he sent me a box of shoes for the children and I realized that he liked me.

Dear Gabby: We miss you very much and hope you have much luck in all your endeavors, whatever they may be. A blessing on your family. Elvira Dirge. Who was this woman?

I think it's important to add this tidbit. I am now recycling soup cans. Shelley came home from junior high one day with a report from her science teacher: "If you can get your family to recycle, I'll up your grade average. Sincerely, Mr. Scanti." Once he gave her detention for not raising her hand to answer a question. So now we have various bags in the kitchen that say RECYCLE CANS and RECYCLE GLASS JARS.

What are condominiums? Large, long, skylighted, angular buildings used to house groups of people; "the poor" and "the middle-income family" and "the middle upper class." Condo dwellers are rarely seen, elusive as leprechauns, they slip to and from work quietly. Probably you know what they look like. Maybe you are one. Maybe you're reading this and chuckling over my ignorance. Ha, ha, ha, you may be saying.

I waited in line for a ticket to the *King Lear* performance at a college, my loud print dress with an old belt around my waist, and I know I looked rather fat and lonely. It was blistering hot and I wondered idly once or twice if I smelled. You know, this is a very odor-conscious society. There I stood, in line with a bunch of beautiful college girls and gorgeous college guys . . . I always feel like a creep when I'm attracted to one of these guys. When I got inside, the auditorium was dark and sweaty, hot already. I sat alone, opening my program and studying who would be in the three-hour play. Lots of beautiful young couples, just back from the Bahamas, filed in. They all had tans and wore light, cool, summery things. I hadn't been able to locate my summer stuff, so I had on a muumuu-type thing that I found out in the back shed yesterday during a hot spell. I was afraid a cute guy would sit next to me, but instead a girl in sleeveless black sat down. I was relieved, frankly, I don't know exactly why. Then when *it* started I began worrying about the kids. I had left them with a sitter but she was new and my kids can be . . . well . . . lively. (Later I found out my son had chased the sitter through the upstairs with a small butter knife . . . not that it could have hurt anybody . . . but sitters freak out easily.)

"Apparently the gentleman has three daughters," I heard someone saying down the row from me. It was a fat man and his crippled wife and their two lovely daughters. "Seems his youngest was the apple of his eye . . . that sort of relationship . . . but, uh . . . from there I don't know . . . it's centered around his youngest, I'm led to believe."

I drove home after the show, listening to the radio. There was an ad on about a rape class. I wondered what they taught. The ad said, "One in three women will be accosted or raped by a man." When I heard that I pulled over and got out, opened all the doors and rattled the seats around, banged around on the floor with a shovel that was in the car, and made sure there wasn't a man hiding in there. He might be getting a free ride to my house where he would leap out as soon as I pulled into my driveway and rape me. But there was no man in the backseat. So I got back inside and drove home.

"The kids were really bad," the baby-sitter said. "They ran away twice . . . and then they called the police and said, 'Come get us! We're trapped down at the old town dump!' Mrs. Fulbriten, do you think I could borrow this peach dress of yours for a week or so? The junior high is having a dance and I need it to wear."

Today I went to the hospital to visit my neighbor Hester, who had the operation and came out fine. The doctors said it was benign and she could go home soon. But I went up to see her to show my support. I bought her a card at the gift shop on the first floor and took a massive elevator to her room. I say "massive" automatically because it rings of hospital talk. The ward was for older folks—not ancient, but older—and I think most of them were bypass surgery, because there were posters on the walls telling you how you would be feeling after open-heart and bypass operations. She was rooming with an exhausted older woman. "Just had a bypass," Hester whispered to me.

The sallow woman's husband stood over her bed and stared down at her. "I'll be right here. I'm not gonna leave," he assured her. "I'm going down the hall to phone the kids. I wanna tell them you're all right. But I'll be right back."

The woman hardly responded. She seemed unable to move, completely without strength. I suppose triple bypass surgery must be exhausting; I don't know. I don't really know what it is, but you hear about people getting it all the time. My quilting teacher's husband got one. The woman beside Hester looked like she was made of wax. Her husband looked a little like wax too as he smiled at us and left the room. "Be right back," he called to her. Her eyelids fluttered. She heaved when she breathed in, her eyes closed and sunken. You can always tell when things aren't going well, because your skin gets sallow. Hester looked a little puffy, but good. She took me in the bathroom and showed me her cut. I call it a cut . . . really, it was a carve . . . it stretched across her back and was stapled together.

"My doctor's going on vacation this week," she said, patting her intravenous-puffy hands together. "He says I'm too much for him. He's going on vacation. I thought he just *went* on vacation."

"They have to do *something* with all their money," I said.

"Hey-yup," she said. "It's going to be strange to miss Saturday night mass. I had the priest here last night, from the bishopry. And this morning two nuns came . . . one nun came this morning and one last night." She breathed in slowly and stood up. "You wanna take a walk? I can show you down the hall . . ."

The sallow woman in the other bed lifted up one long thin arm. "The nun!" she whispered. "The nun this morning . . ." Hester stopped and we waited. "She was drunk!" the woman said triumphantly.

"Drunk . . . why!" Hester looked confused.

"Drunk. They told me you can always tell . . . by the mouthwash they use. She stank of mouthwash." Hester backed away.

"Gee," I said. We couldn't think of anything to say.

"She was weaving and staggering. My father was an alcoholic. I can always tell," the woman went on less sure of herself. Hester looked upset now. I didn't want them to argue.

"Well, that's a shame," I said. "It's a disease, isn't it?"

The woman nodded her head yes. "Maybe I shouldn't have said anything," she said.

Hester urged me with one puffy slow hand to move toward the door. "Good-bye," I called to her. She had leaned back into her pillows and was staring at the ceiling. Hester said, "See down this way? Down here is Stuart Hall . . . see that? It's written on the wall here," and she ran one hand along a plaque. "Hey-yup," she said, holding on to my hand, "I don't know the name of my hall, but this one is Stuart."

Last night, watching Shelley at the high school band performance, I hunched on a bleacher, feeling happy. Here I was with the two smaller children grouped around me, the evening was mild and damp, the band teacher had smiled at us, it seemed nice enough. Shelley leaned forward when she played her saxophone in the beginning band, and later with the jazz band she looked red-faced and afraid. She is less sure of herself on electric keyboard.

What really was going through my mind was all the married men around me . . . I was thinking, "Gee, I could live with that one—he looks clean and pleasant." At this point, clean and pleasant is very appealing. I wondered why all the men I'd met in the past three years were so icky, so horrible. How could there be all these handsome men in one gym in town and none for me? As far as my eye could see, the crowd was all married. Not a single woman loomed from the group save me, and I sat conspicuously on the front bottom bleacher, close to the gym floor. The students played before me, all in black suits and smiling faces. Their fathers and mothers sat in graduated rows of bleachers, laughing and talking with each other. My happiness ebbed. I watched Shelley anguishing out a jazz number. The last concert, she had screwed up by playing the wrong song . . . she was banging out Batman's theme while the jazz band had been playing "Locomotion." It was something that lasted for ten or fifteen seconds before it was corrected, but it remains something to talk about around the school.

"Hi, Gabby," a student says, sauntering past the bleachers when the jazz band has finished their number. "Let's hope Shelley doesn't do it again this year, huh?" I laugh; it's an "in" joke.

But the men don't see me in the gym. I sit for two hours, laughing and smiling and listening to the bands play on, but not a single man looks my way. They look around me and through me but no focus on my face. I am the invisible unmarried woman with the pack of kids.

My mother was a single parent when I grew up in the fifties and sixties. The townspeople used to say, "Jean Fulbriten went in the ditch with Derk Budds." He was the plumber who used to come fix our kitchen sink. My mother didn't like him, but she was so nice to everybody—maybe the town misunderstood. At the time I was only six, so I didn't know what they meant.

Our mother hated for me to go to school after my father died because she was lonely. She said later that it was from irrational anxieties, but I knew it for what it was—she hated sitting at home alone, so she would say in the morning, "Do you feel all right?" and I would say, "Yeah," and she would say, "Lemme see you . . . no . . . huh-uh, you don't look very good to me . . . do you want to stay home? I'll make cookies."

What yearning, what longing for a normal mother! What hope that that would be the normal day I waited my whole childhood for! "Come on, we'll have fun! We can watch *The Beverly Hillbillies.*" At the end of the year she would go into my school, dragging me with her, and say to the teacher, "She's been devastated by her father's death . . . well, yes, we all have . . . but she's going to try to do better next year, aren't you,

Gabby?" and silence while they stared at me and waited for my answer. "Yes, I'm going to do better next year," I'd say.

But you know, my mother had her good points too. She knew Blake poems by heart and would recite them very fast and laugh, throwing her head back like a movie star, always one eye on the mirror. She said funny limericks too, and made up operas in the car when we didn't want her to.

She had a mother whom I knew as "Gram." "I was born in 1882," she'd repeat every few hours. She was a Christian Scientist and she lugged her Bible from room to room as she wandered through our farmhouse, singing black slave songs.

"Mom! Please don't sing that one," my mother would say, her voice cringing.

"Ohhh, my darling Nelly Grey, they have taken you away and I'll never see my darling anymore. I'm a'sittin' by the river and I'm weeping all the day! You have gone from the old Kentucky shore." My mother would cover her ears and rush from the room. Then Gram would give me a huge white-toothed smile—she was in her seventies with perfect teeth, big mouth like a small horse—and say, "The darkies used to sing that . . ." and she'd laugh and begin again.

"Ohhh, oh my darling Nelly Grey . . ."

My mother would be on the porch. "Is she still singing? God, I cry when I hear that song! It's all true, you know. They took children away from the parents; they separated whole families! Jesus God, this world is cruel! Want some crackers and cheese?" She'd point to a plate on a low table, airily, and pour herself more wine. "Awful stuff. I hate Paul Masson," she'd say.

Let's see, I was going to say something nice about my mother. Well, once, I remember, Gram lost her red rose teacup. This is sort of cute. Gram had a teacup she used every morning to drink her tea from. It was white with red roses on it and she called it her red rose teacup. One day, or maybe it was a lot of days in a row, she lost it. Actually, it was every morning.

"Where's my red rose cup?" she'd call, shuffling from room to room in her soft bedroom slippers (which are another story). "Jean? Do you know where my red rose cup is?" It always woke me up. I slept upstairs in our farmhouse in a small room with yellow paint on the walls. I had an iron bed and sometimes I got the feather mattress.

"Hoo-hoo!" she'd call. "Do you know where my red rose cup is? I bet you do!"

So one day my mother found the exact pattern down at the five-and-dime store owned by Hoyt Shuambaum. Mr. Shaumbaum sometimes gave us free paper dolls if we let Mother alone while she shopped. Anyway, she found several shelves of Gram's red rose cup pattern and she bought them all. There were about twenty-five of them. And she brought them home, and the first day she gave one to Gram in the morning, and Gram went off drinking her tea, reading her Bible, smoothing the blanket on her bed. All the furniture in the back bedroom belonged to Gram from the days when she had her own house. That was before we drove down in a rented U-Haul and packed up everything and sold the house. She had to come live with us because she was getting hardening of the arteries.

After an hour or so, Gram misplaced that cup and went calling for her red rose teacup, so Mother brought out another one, and another one, until red rose teacups lay strewn all over the house. And then Gram opened the kitchen cupboard and saw fifteen of them lined up on the shelf. She never called for her cup again.

We were always trying to marry Mother off. I would have been so happy if Mother had only remarried after my father died. But she wouldn't, or couldn't. I realize now how hard it is to get remarried! I mean, God, I can't seem to do it!

I was interested in a painter not too long ago, but he turned out to be so icky! For one thing, he thought he was a reincarnation of a painter who had already died. He thought he had been brought back to fix the dead painter's life. He kept saying, "It's happening. It's happening," and looking psychic. Anyway, he was not my type. I like tall blond guys, and he was gray and bent over. So I sympathize with my mother. I do. I remember how excited we were when she bumped into Larry Shankls again after so many years! His wife had died and his kids were grown—two of them were gay and one was a company head. He had a little Piper Cub that he promised to take her up in . . . Actually, my mother has never set foot in an airplane, but she smiled sweetly at him when he offered. So we thought, "This might be him!" as if he could be the Second Coming. You know . . . I mean, we were that eager to see Mother married again. But as the weeks went on, she dropped little hints: "He drinks all the time." "He doesn't listen to anything I say." "He talks about his dead wife all the time." "He's senile." Well, I can understand. I see the world clearer now than when I was younger. I dated that Rolando Skitchetti, remember? And he seemed sort of handsome; true, his job was a drawback, but otherwise . . . but then he turned out to be . . . unlike me . . . and so . . .

We always knew why Mother couldn't get herself another man (besides the fact that she had three children . . . her husband had died and she was poor) . . . it was because she doubted herself. She would stand in front of the mirror and ask us, "Am I beautiful?" and we would all chime "Yes!" and she'd say, "No . . . I used to be, but I'm not anymore. I've lost my beauty. But I'm a good person, aren't I?" and we'd say, *"Yes,"* and she'd say, "Am I? Really?"

This was what held Mother back. She was basically insecure. "Wanna hear a joke? Oh, you don't. Never mind. Why would you? Do you? Really? Oh, okay."

"So what happened to Larry Shankls?"

"He didn't like me. I know when somebody likes me. He was just using me. Anyway, I think he had hardening of the arteries . . . he told me the same stories over and over. I wasn't going to go up in a plane with someone who couldn't remember simple things! I wasn't going to die for him!"

Last night I dreamed about a man behind a door. He was insistent and almost threatening . . . he was not very bright and not even very good-looking, but very appealing. He was telling me what to do and how to get to another building but I wasn't listening. I ran off without letting him finish, and he was yelling, "No, no, no! Don't go yet!" but he was never visible. He remained behind the door. He was my lover.

I get up longing for a lover. After I send the children off to school I sit at the table and eat strawberries until they are gone. I boil water for tea. I squeeze my hands, trying to wake into reality. Those single overweight women throughout my life were never real to me. The chubby shopkeepers who lived alone after their husbands died; the fat mothers-in-law and enormous neighbors who waddled alone through their lives. Like props in a play, they were nothing more than judicial lighting and shadowy visions. I'm a woman in her thirties . . . longing for man. I'm not past my prime, but mysteriously, men think I am. I watch the lawyers as they drive by. In their uniform cars, on their way to homes outside of town, they look childlike and unmovable. One has curly hair and a sweet, deceptive face, as though he were totally harmless. Maybe I read too much into these men; maybe they *are* totally harmless. Anyway, they can't see me because I am fat, in disguise. I sit behind the wheel of a dirty old Vista with rust on the door. My blackened hair, like witches' strands, hangs across my face, covers my desires. My old black skirt is ripped; my jacket is a lonely check. I lean into the steering wheel to catch the beautiful eyes of a retarded man. His knapsack in one hand makes him look like a college kid, but I know who he is. I would smile at him if he would only see me, but of course I'm not really here, looking out at these sweet relics from my youth—I am really trapped between times, in space, kicking my heels at the time warp.

I am almost thirty-seven, with a shoeful of children—three of them. I'm looking for a wild romance. Nothing permanent . . . well, maybe, but not a prerequisite. Please be tall and strong.

Tall and strong? But what if he was a tall and strong rapist who had bad skin? I mean physical appearance is so basic . . . how can you request physical appearance? Better I should ask for charm. *Men, men, men wanted!* Charming. Humorous. Demanding. Jealous. Gentle. Cruel. *Cruel?* Sorry, no cruels. Would be helpful if you were sort of tall.

Fat women hate one thing more than themselves—fat men. Oh joy! I've found a grain of truth in all this!

The last man I fell in love with was Mr. Marrow, the strange employer whom I spoke to on the phone. He was hiring for a grocery chain and I had some of the right credentials. It's very unusual for a grocery-chain rep to call you, especially after 5 P.M., which it was.

"Hello, I'm with Today and Yesterday food chain. I have your résumé in front of me . . ." It sounded like he was looking at my underwear. "I see you've been working at Double-Coupon Day. Are you free?" His voice was deceptively soft and gentle . . . he sounded like he would melt into the phone, so carefully sweet.

"Free?" I said, frightened out of my wits, and yet very thrilled.

"Could you come to us—if we wanted you?" I said yes, yes, I could come.

"Obviously you're not satisfied with the other company," he said, his voice changing him into a tough businessman. "But we'd like to see if you can *really* work."

I was ironing a piece of material for a quilt top I was making. It was going to be a quilt made of pineapple designs.

"Do you live alone?" he wanted to know. I said no,

but I thought, "What does Today and Yesterday food chain want to know that for?" When we hung up, my brain dripped with his velvet voice . . . Probably he was some horrible fat creep from a back room who chopped lettuce leaves off heads when he wasn't adding the books. But still, his gentle, persuasive voice wouldn't leave my head. It bothered me all through quilting class; all night I tossed in my feather bed, wondering what it was he wanted. And then I didn't hear from him again for a long time.

Actually, the next time I did hear from him it was by letter, informing me that they had filled the position temporarily and if I would like to rewrite my résumé and get a little more experience under my belt they'd be happy to have me in for an interview. His office, the letter said, was two aisles back of the pork display.

When I had a big fight with my teenage daughter, Shelley, a few days ago, I screamed that I was going to call her father and send her down to live with him. "Down" just means wherever he is . . . maybe he's up, but that's not the point. She slammed her bedroom door like on a dull TV show and said, *"Fine! Fine! Get rid of me!"* through the wood. I stared at her door for a minute. She has cut-out pages from magazines taped all over it . . . beautiful young girls from *Seventeen* magazine, all staring angrily into the camera lens, wearing boleros and ponchos and looking unutterably dazzling in a Mexico sun.

"I'm gonna call!" I repeated, and she repeated, *"Fine! Fine!"*

So I called him, her father, a silent banjo-playing computer whiz who lives in some suburb with his new wife. His new wife answered the phone.

"Gerry, your old girlfriend wants to talk to ya," she said. It sounded like she was sneering.

"Ha, there" he said. He still has a southern drawl (I met him in the South and he migrated up to Vermont with me). "How're y'all doin'?"

"We're fine. Gerry . . . I was wondering, could Shelley come live with you . . . for a while . . . you know . . . just for a while . . ." I could hear his new wife in the background calling for her cigarette lighter. They are heavy smokers. I could see Shelley getting sick around all that smoke, plus they live in a kind of scary neighborhood but, well, she'd adjust. After all, she was driving me crazy. It was either her or me . . .

"It'd be better if she came for a day or two at first, wouldn't you think?" Gerry was saying. I recalled when Gerry used to live near us, sometimes Shelley would see him on the street and shout, *"There's Daddy!* Mommy, can't we go see Daddy?" and he would be with his new girlfriend (who later broke up with him) and he would look away from us because he didn't want his friends—his *new* friends—to know he was a father, and I guess he was kind of ashamed of me. "Please, Mommy, there's Daddy. Isn't that Daddy?" And once I said, "I don't think it is—it just looks like him . . ."

". . . there's a bus that only changes once. Golly, it'd be great to see her this weekend. I could take her to my work if she gets here 'fore Friday night . . ."

There were times when I was sorry I'd left him, and times when I was sorry I hadn't given her to him when we broke up. But those were the hard times, and mostly I was glad I had her with me . . . she was a comfort, really . . . when the world seemed to grow bleaker every year.

Not too long ago, when Chernobyl happened, her hair started falling out. I think it was from Chernobyl, but the pediatrician thought it was from distress. I was leaving my husband . . . Well, not really a husband—he was a boyfriend, but we had been together for two years, so I called him "husband" . . . and her hair started falling out. It was all over the bed, and when I brushed her hair it came out in clumps in the brush. I felt so responsible . . . I mean, it was my fault; I left her father (or he left me, actually), and then I broke up with the boyfriend, and Shelley's hair fell out from sorrow. Still, they now say Chernobyl ruined a lot of livestock and deformed all the sheep around Kiev, so maybe it did have an effect on Shelley in Vermont.

"Why don't I give y'all a call tomorrow night and check in about the bus schedule? Leastwise we'll know when she can git here . . . ma wife works in th' evenings, so she'd be here during the day . . ."

I could hear Shelley up in her room cutting furiously out of a magazine. She made one collage after another and hung them all over her room. One of them is on Save the Earth and has a sad-looking beauty from *Seventeen* magazine in the center.

"Okay, then, that's a good idea. Call me tomorrow." I said, and I hung up and promptly forgot all about him.

Recipe for a Man ¤¤¤¤¤¤¤¤¤¤¤¤¤¤¤¤¤¤¤¤¤¤¤¤¤¤

1. *1 X chromosome . . . is it X or XY? Get it right. It wouldn't do to make another woman—we have plenty of those!*
2. *Strong legs, strong arms, strong back, strong personality*
3. *Long bones, but if not long, then lean bones; but barring that as well, then strong*
4. *Jealousy, lustfulness, humor*
5. *Deep knowledge of when to be powerful and when to be laid back. For instance, you wouldn't want him to be overpowering when you are busy.*
6. *Money is of* no *import. You'll realize this as time goes on. He doesn't need to make money to be a hero, but he has to know how to read, how to*

carpenter, how to make love, how to run the family. Am I sounding Mormon?

7. *To make a king, we must act as subjects, fond and pleased with his rulership. He isn't smarter; he is merely ruler. Every little country needs a little king.*
8. *Are you stuck at #6, money is of* no *import? Think on't . . . if he could dig your garden and build your house; if he could trap a raccoon and nab a fish for dinner; what need you of silver coins? (Reason not the need! says Lear.)*
9. *Don't climb all over your man. Think of him as a recipe . . . you put in a little spice and flour, you let it sit. You add some liquid, some sugar, knead it . . . stop . . . let it rise until double in bulk. All recipes with dough need to rest.*

But the recipe for a man is like the gingerbread boy. When he is properly cooked he will be apt to run away. Make friends with the neighborhood animals. Inform them that your gingerbread man may be jogging by in the future; would they keep a judicious eye out for him? Most horses, cows, pigs and foxes will willingly offer to let you know if he passes by their neck of the woods, but when the actual item strolls by, more than likely they'll try to eat him up.

Adequately baked, correctly seasoned, these men don't come in baker's dozens. You're lucky to see one zip by every few years. And even then the whole town is after him and there's little chance of you being the lucky woman. But, of course, it's worth the chase for a man is irreplaceable. He is rare and beautiful. He is the ultimate gift from God.

"A man, young lady! Lady, such a man" (the nurse to Juliet on the subject of Paris, her husband-to-be, in Romeo and Juliet).

Oh love, oh love! It stabs like hot hell knives to be without love. Of course, my mother would say, "But the kids love you. Don't you care about the kids? How are the little dears anyway?" But it changes nothing. I sleep on swords. I walk on molten rock. I eat dirt, and my words and whatever else will go down my neck to fill the void of utter black loneliness. Yeah, I mean it's the pits.

"I mean, don't you even *count* their love? Shelley and . . ."

"Just shut up!" I scream. "I don't mean to be rude, but just shut up!" I think all mothers have made a pact with each other not to understand a thing their kids say to them, even when their kids are in their thirties.

"What's that, honey? You what? Ohh, that's nice . . . mmm," in response to "Where's the masking tape?" Mothers were put here on Earth to irritate; to ruffle feathers and then to soothe.

"I didn't mean anything" most mothers will say when you get mad. "Gee whiz, I'm your mother. Do you think I'd upset you *on purpose*?" Well, no; I'd be a real creep to think *that.*

What are fathers on Earth for? Well, Sundays, for one thing. Shelley's dad left me because we fought all the time. I would like to say it was all his fault and he was a creep, but actually he was sort of nice, if not a bit passive . . . his only big fault was that he was passive aggressive. That's when the man acts like he isn't mad but he can't hear you when you yell at him and he won't do the little things you ask him to do because he forgets. Then when you get mad, he just sits there looking blank, which makes you get madder and madder and he finally gets up and walks away because you have become a screaming banshee that's throwing things. Later you apologize but even then he doesn't seem to respond much, which makes you irritated, and so it goes.

But Gerry left me after four years of fighting and making love. We were very amorous . . . I hate to go into that part because it's depressing to think about when one is single, but we were always in bed having fun when Shelley was a baby. When we broke up, naturally I moved back to my mother's house where I was uncomfortable and lonely, and Gerry found another woman to replace me within one week. That's the way with men. They find some fairly pretty, nice enough woman to live with right away and they get these instant friends and go out together and play cards together and all work in the same damn department together while the bereft woman with kids moves back to her mother's house and listens to people suggest she sue the bastard for everything he's worth.

When we were little, my sister and I pretended it was the end of the world during the winter storms. My mother was always afraid it was anyway. Nine and I would dig tunnels through the deep snow and hide in them and whisper to each other. "It's the end of the world," she would say. "Yeah," I would respond. "All the life on Earth will freeze and die except for the woolly mammoths . . . they will live a little longer . . . and us." This was so scary. To think we were the only ones left alive except for the woolly mammoth . . . "and even the woolly mammoth will be frozen solid . . . walking around looking for food he will be fast frozen in a storm . . ." Mother would call to us from the doorway of our farmhouse in the mountains *"Kids!* Come in before you are obliterated! The snow is coming so fast you won't be able to get back to the house . . . hurry . . . you'll get frostbite . . . you'll be lost . . ." Mother was full of terrifying ideas.

Once, perhaps prophetically, I lived alone in Mother's house with Shelley . . . It was not long after Gerry had left and Mother was on the West Coast writing poetry about Laguna Beach and fighting with some English department . . . She was coming home for Christmas and I wanted to have a big crowd to meet her at the house. But we don't really know anybody in Vermont, so Shelley and I put on snowsuits and mittens and went into the front yard and began making a snowman. We made a huge snowman by the front door . . . and then went on to make eighteen other snowmen all over the yard, waving hello. They all had hats and carrot noses. It was one of those deep snow winters . . . I put bird seed on their heads so when my mother arrived, there were snowmen everywhere with birds on their heads. "Look at all the snowmen!" I said proudly when we pulled up in the yard from the bus station (Mother won't fly). "What men?" Mother wanted to know. "Not *men. Snow*men!" I said. However, she had a point. "Ohh . . . cute," she said. But suddenly it didn't seem so cute. It would have been a lot cuter if there had been eighteen men waving when we arrived. Or even just two. One for Mother and one for me. But Mother insists now she doesn't want a man. "*No* I don't want one!" she shrieks when asked. "I like my privacy. I like my cozy existence. I like to read science books. And astronomy . . . I hate men." Of course we all know that isn't true. It *couldn't* be true. Nobody hates men . . . But then Mother has good reason to hate them. Hers went off and did that terrible thing to her . . . and we weren't even in our own country when he died. She used to say she wanted a carpenter. When we were little we used to ask her, "Mommy, don't you want to get remarried? Please?" as if all she had to do was say yes and we would be a family again. "Oh . . . maybe . . . if he's a carpenter," she would say. And we would be relieved. There was hope. Only we never seemed to meet any carpenters. All we ever met were professors and heads of departments at universities. As a child I had no connection with any carpenters. Mother never hired anybody to do anything around our place. She did it herself. If the water system broke, Mother went out with tools and fixed it herself. If she needed a bookshelf, she built it. Mother had lots of tools . . . in fact, she was a little paranoid about them. If any men dropped in to visit, Mother would later announce she suspected they had stolen some of her tools. We always snickered over this . . . it seemed Freudian to us, her daughters. I never wanted to be like my mother. She was too independent . . . too self-sufficient . . . she would never get a man that way. The way to get a man, I figure, is to *need* one. "Mother, why don't you find somebody and get married? You're going to be lonely when your kids grow up and move away," I said once, trying to be nice.

"Really?" Mother said. "I don't think so . . . I'm not worried a bit. Anyway, where are you planning on going?"

Dignity Divinity

1 father, deserted
1/4 cup sugar
2 cups flour
2 heaping tablespoons children
1 father, disappeared
1 indulgent or disinterested town
1 woman with a weight problem, shabbily dressed
1 or more public embarrassments

All ingredients should be at room temperature. Deserted father should be placed in fry pan first, heated, and left to bolt. Disappeared father and remaining ingredients can be fried slowly with a determined hand pushing the woman shabbily dressed around the pan with brisk movements. Disappeared father should pale and disappear completely by the time sugar begins to burn. Allow public embarrassments to rise to the top and cover the fry pan with a thickened coating of shame. Turn out on floured board and flatten with a tight fist. When hardened this candy can be broken up much like peanut brittle and stored in see-through, no hiding, jars.

Who says I don't have admirers? Why, only yesterday I received two letters from two old admirers. One was from Rolando Skitchetti, who has moved to another state.

"Dear Gabby:

Before I would begin I would ask of you, 'How's it going?" and so forth. Reading through the letter I was struck dumb by how desperate I've become . . . imagining gingerbread lovers! Devising foolproof ways to attract a man! What next? Old Rolando must have sensed the desperation in my driving as I whizzed past the garbage collector hangout. It's possible that I drive like a single parent. Or at least like a woman out of love. Rolando goes on:

> Your work is pretty unusual and interesting.
>
> It would be nice to see you do something else.
>
> How are your kids? Nice to see your children like the printed word as much as their elders.
>
> I make it up your way about once a week. I never notice you around . . . I'd like to say hi and have a cup of coffee.
>
> Anyway, here I am, sitting in my truck. I'm still looking for that "right" job but so far nothing has turned up. I was selling gourmet foods but selling overpriced cholesterol patties didn't appeal to me so I left. Then I tried to sell used cars, but they fired me because I couldn't convince people to buy these suckers. It's been rough going for a while, especially because everybody thinks you have to have a job in order to get anywhere in the world, which I don't agree . . .
>
> I played Trivial Pursuit with a couple of friends, then chess, then poker for a while. An individual whose soul is free like mine is always,

being mistaken for a Commie, just because I am a person of modest means.

I've got a lot to say. I hope we can have that cup of coffee.

Rolando

The only truly inspiring thing about Rolando was his slightly overweight body, which he housed in gross clothes. After I got his letter, I toyed with the idea of trying to fix him up. You know, a lot of a man's appeal is in his strong silence. If I could just get him not to say anything!

Then I also got another letter, from Iggy Stains, who used to live in Utah. Remember I said I was an inactive Mormon? Well, Iggy "found" me when he was a missionary. As a member of the church, if you are a male, you are encouraged to serve a mission somewhere in the world. You pay for it yourself, and you live in a community and try to convert nonmembers into being members. I was living with the three kids on a side street in an apartment in Leadbelly at the time, as an innocent nonmember, when Iggy "found" me.

"I want to teach you the words of wisdom," he said, boring holes into me with his huge, bulging eyes. "I want you to sit down . . . first put out your cigarette . . . now sit down here. There are seven lessons, and I'm going to teach you all of them. Do you know who Joseph Smith is?"

I was riveted by his electricity. He seemed to be charged from above, and driven by sexuality—or by insanity, I don't know. I was, even then, a single parent and it's possible that I was just projecting.

"Here is a picture of Joseph Smith finding the golden plates. I was at the Hill Comorah last month with some other missionaries and it was major cool. Wasn't it, Bill?"

Bill was his fellow missionary who went everywhere with him. Iggy and Bill weren't allowed to be separated for any reason. They even slept in the same room. Bill was very handsome in his dark suit (they all wear dark suits, even in the summer).

"That Hill Comorah was awesome, dude," Bill said. He was playing with my children while Iggy taught me lesson number one.

They came back every night for months, teaching me and playing with my kids. I sang Beatles songs with them and sometimes they brought missionary friends from other wards. They were all striving for the same thing: to go to the celestial kingdom when they died and be able to be with their families throughout all time.

"Through time and eternity. Now isn't that a pretty neat promise? Would you turn down the opportunity to spend eternity with your mom and your kids?" I considered this.

"What about a husband?" I asked.

"God has his plans . . . He's a pretty clever guy . . .

and I think He'll find husbands for all our single sisters when the time is right." This interested me.

"You do?" I said.

"Oh, yes," Iggy went on, "and while you're on this Earth the Lord's church has lots of social events for our single sisters and brothers. In Utah there are even singles wards where everybody in your branch is lookin' . . ."—I considered this—". . . and if you wanted to move out to Utah after you got baptized, I bet I could help you find work, find a place to live. My mom lives there with my little sister . . . she's goin' on a mission pretty soon. I could talk to her about findin' you a place to stay . . . but you gotta git baptized first!"

Iggy's missionary pals were always requesting transfers to get away from him, but they wouldn't tell me why. They just said he was "somethin' else." They all had southern drawls, Utah accents, or maybe Mormon accents. And most of them were very cute and just waiting to get home so they could get good jobs (Mormons make a lot of money) and get married and get their wives pregnant over and over again.

The women in the church they took me to on Sunday all ate chocolate pudding and made Jell-O salads and smiled all the time. They had about ten kids each and sewed and seemed to constantly be pouring Kool-Aid.

"Jesus is your brother," Iggy said. "Isn't that cool? Jesus is our big brother and He loves us. He wants us to be happy. He's just waiting for you to do the right thing. I want you to do the right thing too. And I think you want to . . . it's just the guy in the red suit that's trying to stop you from spending eternity with your big brother and your heavenly Father. All you gotta do is say, 'Hey, let's do it' and I'll take you down."

Iggy meant that he would baptize me if only I would let him. "I want to see you go under, girl. I wanna know you in heaven. Come on! All your relatives on the other side are all saying, 'Do it, do it' 'cause that's the only way they can be saved too is if you go under and then do baptisms for the dead on them. Then you can save them all too. But you do have to give up smokin' first."

Yes, there was something horrifying about Iggy. He was insistent and weird, but I did what he instructed. I took all of the lessons and gave up smoking and drinking and tried to let go of drinking tea.

"How do you get the English to become Mormon?" I wanted to know.

"Oh, they do real good over there . . . it's an easy mission in England. They're just *ready* to go under, believe me. Tea ain't nuthin'. Shoot, I never even had it and I'm not hurtin'."

Anyway, Iggy baptized me at the Joseph Smith Memorial up near Sharon, Vermont, in a blue font, with other missionaries smiling and watching. I had to wear a white polyester dress that went to the floor, and he wore a white shirt and white pants, and we were both barefoot, I think. It was, somehow, very erotic. It was like we were making love in front of these onlookers. He held me with both hands and pushed me down deep in the water after chanting some words and pressing my forehead. I sank straight to the bottom with the force of his hands, and then he pulled me out again and, by God, I felt reborn. Then three men circled around me and by the power of the priesthood (which all worthy men in the Church get from God), they gave me a blessing and anointed me with oil and we all prayed and said "Amen" and I went home singing "When the Roll Is Called up Yonder."

But he calls from time to time and we hedge around whether or not we want to get married . . . whether we like each other *that* way or not . . . and sometimes he writes to me. This letter I just got started out boldly:

"I thought you were going to tell me whether you *really* liked me or not," it began. "But then maybe we're just friends. I wish you'd be honest with me and tell me how you feel about me and the Church." I stopped reading and checked the address. He had joined the army and was living on a base somewhere out west. "I'm still working on base but now I get to *load bombs* instead of just being in the shop fixing things! *Neato!* Well, see ya. Love? Not love? Iggy"

Once he sent me a picture of himself and it seemed like his eyeballs were less intense and he looked, well, kind of handsome. I have often contemplated becoming a devout mother and clean housekeeper, married to Iggy somewhere in a canyon in Utah, bearing child after child and going to hundreds of firesides and social picnics at a local ward. It isn't that I balk at such a picture; I just never get around to writing back to him.

The first time I fell in love it was with the Beatles. I was lying on a floor in someone's house in Massachusetts, watching *The Ed Sullivan Show* on Sunday night. My sister was getting ready to go to a prom at a boys' school. She had a huge pink party dress on and we had come all that way just so she could go to this elite boys' school prom with some date that my mother's friends had fixed her up with. I'm not sure now if she really *wanted* to go or not.

After Topo Gigio, who was my mother's favorite . . . she'd say, "Oh! Oh, Topo! Oh, Topo!" while he was on . . . after him the Beatles came on. And I don't remember the transition between not knowing them and knowing them; between child and teenager; between nothingness and immense joy. I do recall the stiff, off-white rug that I rolled around on, screaming "The Beatles! The Beatles!" After that, I sat in my room playing *Meet the Beatles* and sighing. I cried a lot over them. I loved George Harrison the most, and then John Lennon. When George's album *Wonderwall Music* came out I had grown up pretty much, lying on a mattress on the floor with Indian bedspreads floating everywhere and candles and tarot cards and George Harrison on the turntable. I wore dresses that dragged in the dirt and I loved everyone.

Now I can only see the fab four on VHS movies and somehow it twists the knife of reckoning a little too deeply. My son, J.D., loves them. He is six and watches *Magical Mystery Tour* and *Yellow Submarine* and *A Hard Day's Night* on rainy days after kindergarten. His favorite is Ringo. I am glad he loves Ringo. He points to John's face on the screen when he comes on and says, "There's the one who died, right?" and I say, "Right."

We have to do this over and over, and it makes us sad but we both like doing it.

"There he is," I point out when they are rushing, in *A Hard Day's Night,* toward a hotel. "There's John . . . he got killed."

"Yeah," my son agrees, "he's dead. But that one isn't." And we sigh.

A lot has to leave us. We must sacrifice continually during our lifetimes, and our fondest moments are hardest to give up. Playing "Strawberry Fields Forever" in a cold room when I was thirteen, wishing only for a piece of a towel or blanket they had touched; looking at Beatles cards . . .

When I went to England later, in my late teens, I fell in love with every voice because, to me, they all sounded like the Beatles. When John died, I wept for days. Nothing would ever be the same, nothing—nothing. Here was my youth gone in a bullet, here was my hero turned to nothing. But we heal, and we get over things . . . sort of. I kept the *Newsweek* telling of his death, and I still clip any articles about them . . . but I have relinquished the memories, for the most part, and turned them into something filmy and lost in my back mind. I am working now on recycling soup cans and helping my daughter into her thirteenth year, and wondering what it is between men and women . . . why are we aliens to each other?

I called Mr. Boots, the cowman, this morning because one of the mother cows was mooing and mooing like she had lost her baby. He seemed pleased that I had called, and after an hour or so, his old pickup truck pulled into the field beyond my house.

"Oh Mr. Boots!" I called out, rushing to his truck. His wife, Dorothy Stella, was in the passenger seat and didn't turn around. "I think the mother lost her baby . . . or got sick . . . maybe it's her throat . . ."

Mr. Boots had on a sleeveless T-shirt and was very

tan from working outside on his farm. His large muscles flexed when he bent his arms around his chest.

"I brought her a bull," he said, smiling.

I noticed then that he had a brown cow in the back of the pickup, standing and watching the cows in the field. "You did?"

"Ay-yup. She hasn't lost her baby and there ain't nothin' wrong with her, so I figured she wants to get pregnant. They usually beller when they do . . . he'll fix her up," Mr. Boots said, pushing open the old iron gate that led into the pasture. I retreated, embarrassed.

"She just wants . . . a . . . a . . . boy cow?" I couldn't bring myself to say any more, so I went inside and watched from my window as Mr. Boots led the big brown bull toward the mooing mother cow. I didn't agree with him. I couldn't believe that was all she wanted, but what do I know? I'm no farmer.

I can hear Mr. Boots shouting now. He's screaming, "Lay down, Polly!" and he has the bull on a rope. The bull is trying to run.

"Damn it, Polly, lay down! Oh, damn it!" Mr. Boots shouts as the bull charges and breaks away. Polly chases him through the field, then turns and butts him fiercely. Mr. Boots is disgusted and doesn't want to watch. He's mad that the bull probably gave him rope burns on his big hands. The mother cow, Polly apparently, is mooing terrifically. She rushes through the pasture mooing as though she will split, and the bull

runs pell-mell all over the place. The other cows and their babies are extremely interested in this. They follow Polly and the bull's every move, trotting here and there in an unusual show of energy. Nobody is eating grass.

***

This has nothing to do with cows or mating, but I saw a terrible show on television recently. Actually, I have seen it several times. It's an hour-long commercial, in my opinion. This guy from Vietnam named Don Vu is telling how he got rich in real estate.

"You wanna be rich? I hear so many of you say, 'Yes, Don, I wanna be rich. Yes, Don, I wanna Mercedes,' but nobody do nuthin' about it . . . You all go back to work in the morning at your boring jobs that you no like . . . and get crap for pay. *Why not do what I do? Get rich quick* by buying houses that the bank is repossess. What you care what happens to the people who owned them? Somebody's gonna take it. Might as well be you!"

While he is talking you see on the screen pictures of his family when he was little . . . ten people crowded into one hut somewhere off a rice paddy . . . and then films of Don Vu on his yacht surrounded by partially naked beauty girls who fan him and feed him grapes.

"You wanna live like this? Quit your crummy job. Come work for yourself! I show you how! Get rich quick. I did! See how great I am? I'm successful! Land of opportunity! Here my Mercedes. I got two of them."

The ad for going to Don Vu's seminars on how to rake it in in real estate goes on for about an hour. Mostly all you see is his yacht and his women and the photo of his poverty-stricken family. I wonder if any of the other Vus are still living.

Mr. Boots was back again in his old pickup when I came home today. I had been out getting weighed by my counselor at a diet store. They have diet stores everywhere in town now. I've tried several. The one I settled on is mostly chicken- and tofu-oriented. Some of the other places only let you drink cocoa fluff shakes.

When I pulled into my driveway I saw Mr. Boots roping a calf, and the mother cow that mooed all day was there, mooing again.

"You got any Clorox?" he called out to me from the fence. Well, I don't believe in Clorox because it is one more hazardous liquid that the Earth has to absorb, but I didn't want to appear "earthdayish" to Mr. Boots so I said, "I just ran out . . . but I can get some more. Is something wrong?"

"Calf's got a awful infected foot. *That's* why Polly was bellerin' like that . . . I thought somethin' had to be wrong, 'cause we were drivin' down route eighty and she jumped outa the truck and went lookin' for her baby." He was slowly pulling the calf toward the fence as he talked to me.

"Wow," I said. "So you didn't make her get pregnant?"

"Never even got her back to the farm!" Mr. Boots said. He had pulled the calf up to a fence post and was inspecting its foot. "Well, I couldn't catch her. Then 'bout five o'clock I got a call that she was holdin' up traffic. That time I got her and brought her right straight here . . . she missed her baby. Then I got to thinkin' something had to be wrong with the calf . . . and sure enough, the foot's all swole up and infected, and his eye is infected . . . gee. But I can get him all fixed up if I get some Clorox."

So I went for Clorox and while I was gone the mailman came. I didn't get a letter from Elvira, thank the Lord, but I got a few lawsuit notices on a bad check I wrote at the grocery store. I thought I was secretly the only person who got threatening letters due to lack of money, but I've been told a lot of us here in America bounce checks out of desperation.

"DEAR GABBY FULBRITEN: YOUR CHECK OF $15.00 IS BEING HANDED OVER TO OUR COLLECTION AGENCY."

I fear for Mr. Boots's life. Earlier today he drove on through the gate and headed up to the back pastures to look after his herd. Frankly, I think the baby cow with hoof disease might die. He limped around for two days and the mother seemed to have given up on him entirely. After all that mooing and then Mr. Boots coming with the Clorox, maybe she felt there was nothing else she could do. In any case, she didn't nudge him to nurse or even wait for him when the herd moved on to the lower pasture.

Well, now, Mr. Boots has been out there for close to all day, I'd say, and the way he climbs over the fence and gets right in with them, I'm afraid they've knocked him down in this muddy season and have trampled him by accident. They wouldn't do it on purpose, would they? I think they love him, although when he was here with the Clorox they all clustered around me and the kids and wouldn't give him the time of day. He even remarked on it.

"They like you better'n they do me," he said.

And I said, "Maybe that's because they know what you have in store for them."

"Maybe," he agreed.

But now he has disappeared and I wonder . . . should I call the police? The game warden? Dorothy Stella? Today is Sunday and I'm sure Dorothy Stella is back from church. She's a churchgoing woman, I know.

This worry I have about Mr. Boots fits in with my walk yesterday with Hester. We went down the grassy road toward the back pasture, and when we got to the lower gate the cows saw us. They had been munching quietly, but they mooed wildly and moved in a great rush toward the fence.

"Let's go!" I shrieked, and we both hurried back the way we had come.

"They can't get out," Hester said, running nevertheless.

"That big one looks like he could knock the gate over," I said.

"I don't care if he's been doctored or not," Hester said, slowing up a bit. "I won't walk in a pasture with a bull. Once a bull, always a bull, doctored or not."

It relates to all species, I think. It made me think, "Well, maybe men will come around again. Once a man, always a man." I find a lot of wisdom in my neighbor.

"One of my boys was down today," Hester said on our evening walk. "He said he had a pair of bluebirds in his yard . . . why, I haven't seen bluebirds for . . . years."

I shook my head. "I know, I know!" I said, closing my umbrella and letting the rain fall on me. "I never see bluebirds."

"They say they are . . . well, scarce," Hester explained. She carried her little black umbrella over her head and walked beside me in striped shorts and a white T-shirt. I had been away for a few days and she told me she had missed me. "No one to walk with," she'd said.

"The hummingbirds aren't around anymore either," I said. "That's because the rain forests are being ruined. You know, they don't have anywhere to live. And the songbirds are all dying out from the pesticides . . ."

"Hey-yup," she said. "My boy brought up a mother duck with a stick to shove in the ground, you know . . . and a little baby duck that's white and one that's black, same as she is. They're all wooden and they go in the yard."

We stopped as she said this in front of the gate that led to the river. The river roared through the electric plant and followed the wide bed on through the Vermont countryside, way beyond Leadbelly.

When Hester and I walked home again, we noticed the rain had brought puddles to the road and in the puddles was an oily yellow substance.

"Is it paint?" I asked her. "Maybe it's raining pollution," I said.

"Maybe," she answered. "You finished yer sampler quilt?"

I said I hadn't. I had made a house square and a square of appliquéd flowers. The flowers were in a pink field with green leaves everywhere.

When I was little we used to run barefoot through fields full of Indian paintbrush and daisies. I worry that the wildflowers are disappearing too. I guess I worry too much, but I notice the fields are only full of McDonald wrappers and tough grass, that even the cows seem unsatisfied with the colorless foliage.

I want to tell Hester something funny before we part for the evening, but I can't think of anything. My teenage daughter walks toward us, glaring and holding a purple umbrella. She is full of the empty hours of being thirteen . . . she would like to be recognized but her mother and her brother and sister don't see her for what she really is. Maybe we will, later on . . . or maybe she will tell us to help clarify. Anyway, I only say, "Well, I'll see you tomorrow, Hester. Bye," and I turn to go.

"I put on a little weight while you were gone," she calls to me, "so let's walk every morning, and evening too."

I say okay, I will, but I know I am confused with all the things I have to do. There is so much to do in this culture. We are required to do so many things. I don't know what they are, exactly, but there's a lot of pressure out there to be perfect.

Perfectly Lovely Glace ¤¤¤¤¤¤¤¤¤¤¤¤¤¤¤¤¤¤¤¤

1. A home, so tidy, so clean, so gingham and cheerful, with pots on the walls that you never use, and dishes in cupboards that never fall off
2. A friendly husband who works at a wonderful job and wears checkered warm shirts and builds

porches in the evenings. He laughs a lot and hugs you while you prepare dinner.

3. *Children who never glare*
4. *A beautiful body, thanks to aerobic classes at the local health club. You work out with all the other good-looking married women in town. They laugh with you while you shower and dress in your clean, crisp, size 8 clothes.*
5. *A dog that doesn't smell or pee on the floor; a fluffy cat that doesn't urinate on your quilt pieces*
6. *An appetite that doesn't border on the psychotically voracious*
7. *A cheerful, rewarding job that lets you vacation a few times a year with your hubby in warm climates*

Cookbooks always relax me because I can walk through them with my longing eyes and devour all the recipes and calming instructions and descriptions without ever dirtying a dish.

Hester and I sat out in front of her house this evening with one of her grown daughters and watched the traffic go by. She has three lawn chairs set up near the road, and we commented on the police sergeant cruising by several times, going down to the condos.

"Must be trouble down there somewhere," Hester

said, and her daughter and I agreed. "He was down there the other night too." We nodded. Something was fishy, but what we might never know. Those condo dwellers were a shadowy threat to us.

Hester's daughter had a little lap dog with her that barked every time a car went by.

"Boy, this is nothin' like it used to be, Ma," the daughter said, shaking her head at the huge camper van that pulled into the drive across the road.

"I know it," Hester said.

I leaned back in my lawn chair and sighed.

"I saw some milkweed down at the dump," I said. "That gives me hope about the monarch butterflies. You know they depend on milkweed to survive. I thought it had disappeared, but there were two stalks down there this morning."

"This neighborhood was quiet as a mouse when I was growing up," Hester's daughter explained, leaning over Hester to look at me. "At night when you went to sleep you didn't hear a thing."

"That's right," Hester said. "Why, hardly a car would go by. Very rarely would a car go on through . . . It was quiet out here."

Hester looked out at the condos down the hill from us. A woman in a tennis dress was heading our way, walking barefoot along the grass.

"Well, Tink would shoot his gun," the daughter corrected.

"Hey-yup, he did." Hester said.

The daughter looked at me. "Tink would go out in the yard some nights and shoot a few bullets."

"Yeah," Hester said. "When he was feelin' good he'd shoot his gun and run over his dog. That's what he'd do if he was feelin' good . . . get drunk and run over his dog."

"Regular neighbor . . . nothin' special," the daughter added.

"Hey-yup. Not like it is now."

We bought a new bowl for the fish. It's much bigger and holds a lot more water. We bought it a friend too, but the friend died. The friend was named Antony, and Shelley made Antony a gravestone out of wood blocks and buried it in the backyard while the two younger children watched. They cried when they covered Antony with dirt.

"Now he's really dead," J.D. said, shaking his head. "I thought I saw him move when he was in the water, but now he's never going to wake up . . . not with all that dirt on him!"

J.D. found a worm on our front porch later in the day and lay down next to it.

"I wish wish wish I was a worm," he told me. "I know this worm is telling me something . . . very important . . . but I can't understand him. It's all worm talk. Oh, I wish I could be a worm!"

I'm afraid he's just saying that because his aunt told

me his father was a real worm, and I think J.D. heard her say that. That's my oldest sister, for the record. J.D. has never met anyone on his father's side. Anyway I don't agree. His father wasn't a worm, but J.D.'s aunt is very opinionated, especially about the men in my life. If you want to know the truth, my family never liked my husband—or the boyfriends I've brought into the fold. They always think the man is trying to steal me away or will eventually steal the children away. Though I know it can happen that there will be an ugly custody suit, my own feeling is that my family doesn't want me to have a man so they can keep a firmer grip on my life. I'll say, "I wish the kids could know their father," hoping they'll say, "I do too. Why don't you write to him again."

But what they always really say is, "You idiot. You ass. You fool. Thank *God* he doesn't have anything to do with any of you. I'm just scared to death that he'll come around and try to steal J.D. . . . I mean, what with that powerful father! Those powerful relatives in high places . . . they look like mafia to me! You never know. Stay away from him. Don't be an idiot. The kids don't need a father, they need you!" and so on.

I don't mean to sound bitter or hostile, though I guess I am. I want to remain somewhat lighthearted about the whole state of affairs in our world now, but it's disconcerting nonetheless that you have to tiptoe around, scared to death that someone will steal your heart out of its sleeve—you know? I mean, what could my children's father really do? Take me to court and remove the children from my home? Take them to a foreign country and never let me see them again? Well, if he was Donald Trump I guess he might. But I think the chance of good old whatshisname showing that much enthusiasm is slim. And should we fear my old boyfriend so much? Is he so dangerous? So frightful? I remember him as thin and childish. He was a vegetarian who cried a lot.

Actually, there are quite a few women around here who have decided to leave their children with the fathers in a divorce. Somehow I feel we've already been over this point, but let's reiterate. One woman I know of left her husband for a guy I later ended up with—she left her husband and both her children, even though they were small, and went to work in a building next door to their school. When the children came out of school every day she would be coming out of work. They would call to her—"Mommy! Mommy!"—and she would wave but she wouldn't go see them. She was gone, man; I mean, she was *out* of there.

Last night when I took the kids to the fireworks display on the lake, we stopped at a country store to get Cokes and I thought I saw one of her boys in the store and I said, "Well, hi, Billy, how are you?" and the boy said, "Fine," and I thought, "Gee, Billy is looking all right. I guess losing his mother didn't wreck him." Then when I took the Cokes to the car, I said to Shelley, "There's Billy."

And she said, "Mom, what a dork! That's not Billy; that's Tommy Falbrooker. He played Friedrich in *The Sound of Music* last summer. Remember? God, you thought that was Billy?"

"Yes," I said, mortified. "I even said 'Hi, Billy' to him and he said 'Hi' back. No wonder he looked so good. Tommy Falbrooker is that brilliant kid who's already a concert pianist at the age of nine—right?"

"God, Mom," Shelley said, "I have *no* idea."

Anyway, there you have it in a nutshell. No point in trying to cheer people on or up or anything because they probably aren't who you think they are anyway. You say, 'Hi. I feel for you. I understand' and what happens? They turn out to be Tommy Falbrooker instead of Billy Pinkerton. C'est la vie.

Some women, when getting divorced—or changing horses in midstream, as it were—will take *half* the kids. They might take the ones, say, from a previous marriage and leave the newer marriage kids to the husband; or they might take the littlest boy and leave the bigger boy for the father; and so on. I know one such child. The mother took the younger son and gave the older son to the father, who was leaving with another woman who was pregnant with his child. So the children can be split like thus:

Families on the Half Shell ¤¤¤¤¤¤¤¤¤¤¤¤¤¤¤¤

1. 1 angry man, 1 angry woman (all the fury is probably coming from Chernobyl)
2. A round, sweet dewdrop child; an older, more solemn sibling; an infant
3. A car, a bank account, some life insurance, a dog

Put the dog in the car with the older sibling and the life insurance. Cut in the father with a pastry knife. Form into balls and freeze. Now place mother, infant, and dewdrop baby with the bank account. Mix until all dough disappears.

The summer is hot. And though I see Hester going back and forth along the wildflower roads on her afternoon walks, I do not go with her. I am waiting for something. I am waiting for my sunflowers to grow. And for my flowering crab to take hold and bear fruit. I am waiting for my yard to blossom and spring up into something wonderful. And I am waiting for a fella.

This morning I drove up along the mountain and filled the car with sand from a sand pit. I stopped at a nursery and bought a happy, shrubby rose. I took the younger children to day camp. And I listened to the fuming of my older daughter . . . how unfair I was. How awful her hair is. How gross this guy in saxophone day camp is. When I was alone in the car with the wind whipping through the thorns of my rose shrub, I pulled over and bought a huge chocolate sundae at a Creemee stand. Then I listened to *Romeo and Juliet* as I drove. Ice cream dripped down the front of my muumuu. Boxes of sand slid from one edge of the car seat to the other. I saw men working on the roads, men clearing brush on the highway, men fixing pipelines in town, men driving tractors in the fields . . . but no men for me. The ice cream was good; I almost went back for another round, but I could see the flowery shrub in the backseat was withering fast . . . these frail flowers need a place to call home as soon as possible . . . otherwise they collapse and just don't have the oomph to bother going on.

I played the part in *Romeo and Juliet* over and over where he hears her talking about him on her balcony. She's out there in the middle of the night saying how swell he is . . . "Romeo, doff thy name," she says, meaning: don't be a Montague—be something else so she can be with him. She's out there swelled with love, and he's down below, listening, like a thief . . . He hears this great stuff about himself. She says, "Take me; take me!" and he bursts with affirmation all over the place. They speak for a long time. She says she wishes he could be her little bird . . . like wantons have (What are wantons?), and she says she'd keep him on a string; and he says "Okay, do that," and she begs him to marry her and he says, "Yes. Yes," and then Nurse calls to her and she can't talk anymore . . .

but they go on talking anyway . . . and the tension rises and he is so full of love for her he can hardly do more than answer yes to whatever she says . . . and she . . . oh, well . . . it's such a good part. I listened to it again and again, with vanilla Softee running down my dress front and chocolate on my chin, like the disabled lonely heart that I am. Did I cry? Well you might ask. No, I did not. I cried the first fifteen times I heard it, but this time I just sighed and felt a lump form in my throat. I could see the men up ahead on route 6 flagging me down as I approached some road work. One guy stood right in front of my car—fearless, like before a bull in the ring, holding his red flag—and shirtless, staring into my windshield. I smiled shyly and looked away quickly. I feared he would point and guffaw. I would never be good at confrontation combat sort of work. I am just too self-conscious anymore.

Well, today really is a broiler. I think some nice cool dish would do for dinner, and I think I will insert a cooling recipe for a hot day at this point.

Maleless Brunch ¤¤¤¤¤¤¤¤¤¤¤¤¤¤¤¤¤¤¤¤¤¤¤¤

1. *Several single mothers—on the unattractive side, slightly overweight, or perhaps with bad skin (maybe a few who are too thin and who make a lot of boring conversation about when they used to be waitresses)*
2. *Diet Coke, glasses (Tupperware, if you please)*

and even a Tupperware representative with an assortment of plastic containers for you to look through

3. *Tablecloth, napkins, fruit compote—or just peaches in a bowl*
4. *Sandwiches*

Hire a man with a bulldozer if possible, to ride around the edge of your property shoving down weed trees and wrenching roots right up out of the earth like Hercules or something. He will be bound to take his shirt off if you planned your brunch on a sweltering day. Say to one of your company, "He reminds me of a guy I used to go out with." Let the conversation jell until set. Serve cold. Bag leftovers.

Recently I dreamed the grocery-chain representative offered me a few hours of bulldozer work. I said, "Oh, good, now I can have a garden dug." I couldn't see him . . . he was still on the phone, but his voice was powerful—like a John Deere—and he was offering me something. When I woke up in the morning, I went into town happily. Sometimes if you can't get what you need during your day, your dreams will supply you with it at night. I was headed to the Hallmark shop where I could spend some time browsing through cute cups with sayings on them. They don't like you to finger the cards, but I did want to take a peek at some of the religious ones to see if Elvira Dirge was a local and bought the blessing cards at

Hallmark. All of a sudden Billy Pinkerton approached me and held out some tickets.

"Wanna buy a raffle ticket?" he asked. I was really taken aback.

"Sure I do," I said. "I'll take four." He wrote my name four times on the tickets and I gave him four dollars.

"Thanks a lot," he said, moving away.

"What do you get if you win?" I wanted to know.

He smiled. "It's kinda dumb," he said, "but it's four hours of bulldozer work."

> SINGLE MALE LOOKING FOR WOMAN. MUST BE ENTHUSIASTIC, READY FOR POSSIBLE COMMITMENT. TOBACCO-FREE; LIGHT DRINKER. I LOVE SKIING, TENNIS, INDOOR SPORTS, CYCLING, HIKING, CROSS-COUNTRY, WATER SPORTS. I AM PHYSICALLY FIT AND TRIM AND SEEK SAME. COME ON! I KNOW YOU'RE READING THIS! CALL.

Why do I feel so unsuited to the needs of the new man? I came from the era that learned how to make Indian curry soup and toast soybeans in the oven. I can decorate my man's VW bus or polyurethane the wood floors of his cabin in the woods. I can read him *Siddartha* at night under the stars; I can make love like the delicate, passionate, wild—yet obedient—female I am wont to be. But the only rugged cycling I do is recycling. And I hate indoor sports and long hours on skis. Trim? That's what you do to hair. It's a noun, not an adjective. Where are the men who long for love? Why do they seek an opponent now instead of a female?

Several days after running into Billy Pinkerton, I got a phone call.

"Gabby Fulbriten?"

"Yes."

"Gabby, this is Buster's Refurbishing Construction."

"Did I bounce a check? It was the bank's fault . . ."

"Gabby, you're the grand-prize winner! You won full use of one of our bulldozers for four hours! How about that?"

I was standing in the piano room and Shelley was playing Tarantella on the piano. But I heard nothing except my own joy-filled voice saying, "Thank you, Buster. It's just what I've always wanted . . . really . . . you can't know . . ."

"I'll send Joe out in a few days . . . how 'bout that?"

I said, "Yeah, how about that?" God, how about that? "I can't believe this," I said.

So not only was I getting my garden; I was now a psychic. Maybe I could sell my dreams to desperate women who sought things in their own lives?

Everyone in town now has a blue plastic box in front of their house. This is our town's way of trying to save the world—through recycling soup cans and glass jars and newspaper. At first it was exciting. I washed and scrubbed each cat food can, every orange juice bottle.

J.D. got the job of trucking things out to the blue box. We all were actively involved. But then the novelty wore off and Earth Day passed and we are left with the reality of having to do a lot more dishwashing than before. Who wants to scrub filthy cat cans every day? But still our Earth sickens. I know it to be true. We live not too far away from a sewage treatment plant. God knows what they actually do there, but the stench that rises and floats along our street once a day is horrendous. Some evenings, when the birds are putting themselves to bed with songs, and the garbage trucks down the road are running their motors, idling but not driving around, and the condo dwellers are all home from the Kraft factories, and the heat of the greenhouse effect is somewhat lessened by the oncoming night, the stench rises from the sewage treatment plant and fills the evening with rank truth—we have ruined our planet. Shame, shame, shame on us all. Shame on the juice box companies and on me for buying the kids juice boxes to take to camp. Shame on the plastic diaper companies and the condo makers.

Back in the old days, I was thinking, they had regular wars to kill the men you know, bayonet-type wars—and the women all died in childbirth. The children were killed off with strep throat and other handy illnesses and the world was not overfull. They didn't need special plants to grind up our excrement . . . they just dug a hole. Imagine how many outhouses New York would need!

Oh, that this too too solid flesh would melt,
Thaw, and resolve itself into a dew!
—Hamlet

Anyway, I make out that this place is so grand, out here among the peaceful cows and my good neighbor Hester . . . I mean, I just touched on the fact of the old town dump's being out here and the garbage trucks lined up a few hundred yards down the road and the sewage treatment plant half a mile away . . . To be perfectly honest, this area could use some help. I mean, when the bulldozer came and dug out a huge area for my garden, we discovered half the earth under the grass cover was glass and metal. I found antique blue bottles and ancient perfume vials . . . and when I planted my spinach and lettuce and carrots and peas, and watered them and watched them like a caring gardener, I discovered I had a garden of glass. Things came up, but with them came shards and plates and knifelike ridges of glittering glass. So when I water my garden, the glass sparkles and the beans grow. But will I dare eat anything?

A few days ago Shelley's Dad arranged to meet us halfway to Boston and take Shelley for the weekend.

"Ma wife is off campin' with some friends and me an' the boys are here alone . . . thought it'd be a good time for Shelley t' stop down."

So we decided on a halfway spot, and Shelley packed her duffel bag with her camera and notebook and swimming suit.

"How 'bout that bridge over in Quechee?" he asked me. "You know the one . . . where the guy fell over the edge last year?"

"I know the one," I said, "but it wasn't that he fell over . . . he was pushing his ex-girlfriend and she wouldn't let go of him and they both went over . . . it's a long way down . . ."

"Right . . . well, let's meet there . . ."

"And another time some guy shoved his whole family over the edge . . . and that's where they found the abandoned car where they suspect the nurse was pushed in too."

It was all coming back to me . . . I hadn't been to Quechee Gorge Bridge since I was little when my mother used to shriek *"Ew-w-w-w,* don't look down!" as we sped over the precipice to the safe town of North Quechee. But we always looked . . . and from inside the car windows we could see the fathomless, bottomless cavity of earth that yawned beneath the bridge trestles . . . where way down at its endless bottom there ran a cold brook.

"Jesus God I wish we had come over 103 instead," Mother would say. "I hate this goddam route 4 . . . it's deadly."

When Shelley and I pulled into the parking lot

before the bridge, he was there in his maroon bomb, smiling.

"Ha, there," he said, getting out. "Shall we go look over the edge?"

We did. We leaned over the railing only slightly and watched the little river pour over tiny rocks below. Some wise guy was walking along the railing and jumping out now and again in front of traffic.

"We better get started," he said, and we eased back over the bridge to our cars. We were the only people who didn't have a camera with us.

"Please take care of her. Don't let anything happen to her," I said. It sounded stupid and he looked at me as though I was embarrassing him to say it, but he said, "Oh, I will." I hugged Shelley and she hugged me and she hugged her father and I drove away, listening to *Hamlet* on tape all the way through Woodstock, Pittsfield, and onward over route 100 . . .

"Oh, God! God! / How weary, stale, flat, and unprofitable / Seem to me all the uses of this world! / Fie on 'it, ah, fie! 'Tis an unweeded garden / That grows to seed, things rank and gross in nature / Possess it merely. That it should come to this!"

I woke to the throng of birds that now are housed near my bedroom window, and went out to my glass garden. Between the rows of brown and green glass stood sturdy stalks. I guess the raccoons came in the night and stripped the leaves off everything. I thought, "How sad. If they had only waited, their dinner would have been all the larger." . . . By the end of July the beans would have made a tasty treat. Rushing before it was ready, they ruined it for everyone . . . probably one mean raccoon did all the damage, and now all the raccoons must suffer. One night when we came home early we saw six raccoons in our garbage. When they saw the headlights of our car, they trundled like a six-piece band, in file, up our popple tree, and there they hung, staring down at us with bright eyes, swaying on their perches, waiting for us to go away. And we obliged, most certainly, because I had heard on the radio that day that there were rabid raccoons scouring the countryside, biting little girls who strayed from their yards. We went inside, locked both screen doors and bolted the door. We could hear them from the kitchen, rustling and snapping, chewing and hurrying around, flinging papers all over the yard. In the morning it looked like there had been a raccoon reunion . . . a birthday party for the forest beasts. Cat food tins and hamburger packaging was strewn in my flower beds . . . coffee grounds were littered along the walkway. It was kind of scary.

Buttery Brazen Beans au Naturel ¤¤¤¤¤¤¤¤¤¤¤

2 cups dried navy or white beans
1/2 pound Italian sausage, cooked (or wild raccoon if you prefer)
2 large onions, chopped and sautéed in butter with garlic clove
2 teaspoons dried mustard
3/4 cup Vermont honey
Enough water to cover beans throughout cooking
Corrected seasoning, freshly ground black pepper and salt
1/2 cup butter

Wash and soak beans for 3 hours. Add to pot of boiling water and simmer till somewhat soft. Drain, turn into pot into which all other ingredients, except butter, are simmering. . . . If using raccoon, cover and allow to boil all day; otherwise, check simmering beans every half hour or so, and when they are well done and delicious to taste, add butter, allowing it to melt over beans. Serve while listening to some brass ensemble.

Thought it would be of interest to mention: got another letter from Elvira Dirge. "You have a very, very nice family. A blessing from Elvira Dirge. P.S. We would like to visit you." This puzzled me. "We?" Were there several Elviras?

When I went back to pick up Shelley on the Quechee Gorge Bridge, they were sitting in the car, smiling. But when she got out I saw there was a huge lump on her head and dried blood in the center.

"What happened? To your *head*!" Shelley rushed to me.

"Mom, stop. Stop. I won't come home with you if you don't cool it. It was nothing."

"She got X rays of her head at the hospital," her father said.

"It was one of his new kids . . . playing around . . . the baseball bat hit me. The doctor said I was all right. *Mom!"* Shelley glared at me. Her head was swollen and her eyes seemed foggy.

"There's nothing much wrong . . . They checked her out real good." He was standing close to me. I could have reached out and hit him . . . but we just got in the car and drove home. I screamed and yelled some but now I have gotten over it. I have brought her up . . . for thirteen years she has never been beaten with a baseball bat, granted it was an accident . . . but she was only there two days. And what made it more strange was they weren't even playing baseball . . . the boy was just swinging his bat at her.

Being Soup ¤¤¤¤¤¤¤¤¤¤¤¤¤¤¤¤¤¤¤¤¤¤¤¤¤¤¤

Soak your feelings overnight.
Rinse in cool water, rubbing off any excess.

Add to water containing 1 or more necessary ingredients.
The body of the soup must be of sturdy consistency.
Aroma should be heady.
Just before serving, cut to the chase.

Some Recent Problems

My mother turned yellow for three weeks and had a terrible time eating anything. She lost twenty pounds. I hung around her, trying to help, and possibly even catch the disease. You know anyone who could go through Medifast, Diet World, Weight Watchers, and hundreds of other diets would be willing to try "Get yellow, lose weight" . . . but she got over it and I stay fat.

Also, I got some awful-looking lump above my eye that I tried to get rid of by bothering with it, you know . . . and it got infected and my face swelled up to match my stomach. What a sight. But I'm getting over it.

And then one day my younger daughter brought home clams or mussels from the lake on one of her camp trips. The little kids go to day camp and day camp is always taking them on interesting expeditions where they discover wild small animals. She brought them home in her pocket. They were alive.

"Get the old fish bowl! The old one! We don't want to infect the fish by putting them in with it . . . do we? I don't think we should! Get the old small bowl!" I shouted instructions and got very upset. We put them in the old bowl with some fish food thrown in for good measure . . . and she also brought some tiny snails with her, so we put those in too. For three days the clams or mussels stayed closed and looked rather okay . . . then one day it began to smell a little. I thought the cat had peed in the room. Then a white slippery substance came partially out of the clamshell . . . it seemed dissatisfied with what it saw and by the end of the day had gone back in. The other one didn't open up at all. Three more days and the room stank. The snails had died and the mussels were opening up again. We all wanted to take them back to the lake.

The children wept and said, "We'll help take them back!" and I wanted to oblige . . . but one day slid into another . . . day camp and quilt class . . . the white thing would come out . . . and go in . . . the water was rank. We murdered them. Finally I dumped them in the garden. One clam was really out and dead . . . the other seemed to have just discovered its plight. There is something about the urgency of my surroundings and the accompanying apathy.

One night I was staying up really late, working on my sampler quilt. I had been half-heartedly hoping the grocery-chain rep would call me again . . . I had heard he might be moving to another location somewhere out of state, and I was hoping he would hire me before it was too late for me to know him. You know, I've never even talked about my ability to check out. I'm one of the fastest checkers in the business, but because of all my kids, well, I haven't been able to keep steady work.

I was in my sewing room when I heard this screaming noise. I went into the hall and looked out onto the porch . . . There was a raccoon hanging on my porch screen.

Shelley called downstairs, "What's that noise?"

"It's a raccoon," I said. "What are you doing up?"

"Reading. Where's the raccoon?"

I looked out again. It was swinging on the screen now, shrieking. There was more noise coming from the garbage cans outside.

"I don't think I have any garbage in the can, guys," I said.

But the racket went on, and there seemed to be another raccoon now on the other end of the porch. It began to look like they were trying to get in to *us*.

"Hide! Get upstairs! They're after us!" I shouted. The raccoons screamed more.

"Mom, go see what they want," Shelley said.

So I took a flashlight and went out onto the porch. I made shooting sounds.

"Bang! Bang!" I yelled at them. They shrieked back at me and clung to the screen. The sound kept coming from the garbage can, but it was a scratching sound.

"One is stuck, I bet," I said. I opened the screen

door, saying, *"I'm coming out! I'm on my way out! Get out of my way!"* I had a broom with me . . . Why do people always grab brooms when they're in trouble? It must date back to an earlier time when the broom was a more powerful weapon. *"I'm out! I have the broom!"* I continued to shout. The raccoons on the porch screen hurried away and hid behind my old VW bus parked in the yard.

That's one of my old dreams up on blocks: to travel cross country again in the VW, camping and making love under the stars. But the bus is rusted through completely under most of it and wouldn't start to save its life, and besides, I have no one to make love with under the stars even if I got the old relic on the road.

But the raccoons hid there. I went to the huge barrel by the road that I use as a garbage can and peeked in. A baby raccoon was drowning in it. I took the broom and pushed the barrel over and went screaming into the house, *"Open the door! Let me in! It's coming! Hurry!"* And sure enough, it chased me across the yard. It must have thought I was its mother or something . . . maybe the flashlight reminded it of its mother's eyes. But I got away and they didn't bother our garbage for almost a week after that.

The baby had looked very wet. I was amazed that the parents had been smart enough to hound me into saving it . . . that they had trusted me enough. It was cute, like the clams were not. I guess one thing evens out another. Save a coon, kill a clam.

Horror Tostadas ¤¤¤¤¤¤¤¤¤¤¤¤¤¤¤¤¤¤¤¤¤¤¤¤¤¤¤¤

1. *Slippery white substances, straining for life*
2. *Big clawing wild rodents reaching toward you*
3. *Drowning, wet children rodents calling you*
4. *A yellow mother who languishes*
5. *Layers of lard covering your personality, obliterating your face, sunken in fat, swollen eye*
6. *Garbage all over the lawn*

Using a partially dampened shell, roll all ingredients into one frightening lump and seal with a pick. Layer several of these onto a cookie sheet and burn in hot oven till one thing has melted into another and all the horrors are equal and unrecognizable in every bite. Makes single serving for single person. Top with unrelenting loneliness.

I can laugh about it now. The two-week-long vacation to Washington—the first night on the road when we stopped at a budget motel.

"Do you have a room?" I asked the man at the sleazy desk. He was talking to someone in the other room and swatting flies.

"How many you got with you tonight, sweetheart?" he wanted to know. I thought he was being parental or something.

The room itself (I always ask to inspect the room first) was okay . . . no air-conditioning, but there was a big bed and a TV . . . but when the kids and I were walking back to tell the man we'd take it, a woman in small clothes sauntered by with two guys zipping up their pants. I mean, I thought prostitution was all but obsolete, with AIDS . . . and here were these two rather nice-looking guys, zipping up their pants behind her, and she was telling one of them, "I got a dentist appointment, honey. Don't you know that? I have a very urgent dentist!" and then she laughed and the guys hurried off.

There was this pretty woman with *two* guys, and I can't get one. Actually, that wasn't my reaction at the time, but now that I think of it, that seems to be the most important factor.

We didn't take the room, of course, with hookers coming in and out all night. I might not have gotten any sleep. But there was this woman . . . with *two* guys. I could just cry. How does she meet them?

It never occurred to me to try to be a prostitute. Prostitutes have to keep switching guys and I don't want that. I just want one, or maybe two, over a period of, say, a couple of years. Anyway, this is all irrelevant. Back to the vacation with the kids.

On the Bridge into Baltimore

Car broke down on middle of bridge. Just refused to keep moving. Panic in car. Kids looking fearfully out windows as semitractor/trailer trucks roar by, some of them beeping. As if I could get out of the way! I'm standing beside the car with the hood up, looking like a dumb chick, I suppose. Nobody stops. But I didn't expect them to . . . it's a dangerous bridge and there's no real place to stop and anyway, I'm fat and I know it, and my three kids are grubby after two days in the car, and my bumper stickers say IT'S NEVER TOO LATE TO HAVE A HAPPY CHILDHOOD and DON'T KILL THE ELEPHANTS. All in all, we aren't exactly an appealing, sexy pickup. We look more like the Okies probably looked. Policewoman stops. She's really nice. She pushes the car off the bridge, down the ramp and into a police station. Cute policemen are everywhere. I'm feeling a little better.

What the Policewoman Told Me

"I can talk to you, honey. I know I'll never see you again is why. But I'm so upset . . . You probably heard me in the station, talking to that man on the phone . . . they're saying I have to meet with the authorities about my babies. My kids are fine, but—you know—I have to work from three P.M. till midnight and the kids stay alone during that time. What else can I do? I'm divorced, like you . . . you are, aren't you? Yeah, I thought so. Well, my daughter is twelve; she's old enough to watch the six-year-old. But my sister-in-law called the state authorities and said my son was afraid to go home because he had to be alone with his sister and he was scared. Well, can you believe that? I never once hit my kids . . . I never did anything! I mean, we all sleep together even! Do you think that's weird? I don't get to be with them enough, you know? I mean, they're in school . . . they're at the sitter's . . . they're off here and there, and then I work. So we sleep together . . . all of us in one big bed. I love my kids. They shove me off the bed four times a night! My daughter says, 'Ma, you need to lose about twenty pounds . . .' She's ashamed of me. But that's the way they are at twelve, y'know? God, sometimes she really gets me confused. But do you think I sound like a bad mother? *Am* I a good mother? I always thought I was . . . and now I have to go talk with these bimbos about my parenting because my sister-in-law said I was neglecting them by leaving them alone. I love my kids! That's why I'm working! I don't care if they're in fancy clothes or not, you know? It's love that's important . . . but now I gotta go talk to this woman and I'm afraid I'm gonna explode. I feel like I'll punch her lights out, you know? I have a horrible temper. Better not mess with me and my kids."

Now there's this big war in Iraq . . . or maybe there is. While we were on vacation I listened to *The MacNeil/Lehrer Report* in a hotel room (we ended up in a Howard Johnson's with a lot of normal moms and dads) and according to Mr. MacNeil or Mr. Lehrer (I can't tell them apart), President Bush didn't exactly help matters when he made King Hussein wait in

Washington for a whole day or two before Mr. Bush could see him. Maybe the president was en route to Kennebunkport in his car loaded with sleeping bags and banana peels, like we were, and couldn't get together with the king for that reason, but probably he was making a point. Anyway, here we are in this scary war . . . who knows what will happen? Maybe Saddam Hussein of Iraq has nuclear weapons and just isn't telling us. Maybe he will get Iran to join with him and they'll blow us all away. Maybe we will obliterate Iraq and Iran. I like the way President Bush diminishes President Hussein by calling him "Sad-Am."

I used to know a lot of Arabs myself. One guy I just loved was named Fairydoon. He was so cute and he seemed really to love me too . . . I mean, he was teaching me his language and I was learning . . . and then one day he backed me into a wall on a side street late at night and said, "You see . . . you . . . me . . . this can no be . . . you are Christmas. *I* am MUSLIMAN."

During newsreels now on *The MacNeil/Lehrer Report* I look for Fairydoon's face amongst the angry men they show all over the Middle East. I search these clippings for him but I sort of have forgotten what he looks like. Anyway, he would have gray hair by now.

SINGLE ATTRACTIVE WOMAN SEEKS WAR VET TO CARE FOR. I GIVE TLC. BIG ESTATE WITH POOL AND GROUNDS FOR YOU TO ENJOY. MUST BE MISSING BOTH LEGS.

On our vacation we went to Washington, D.C., and saw the Vietnam Wall. It is shiny black so at first you cannot see anything but your own reflection in it . . . then the names begin to appear, hundreds and hundreds of names of men. These are all the men who died in the Vietnam War ("nam" backward is "man"). There are books with plastic covers nearby with the names in alphabetical order and their addresses so it is easier for you to find a certain name. And they have the addresses because there were a lot of men who died who had the same name and so they are each represented. On the walk along the wall there were a few roses strewn here and there . . . some carnations, and a teddy bear. It was raining. The kids were running their hands along the smooth black granite with bumpy names and Grace said, "These are all dead people? Look, J.D., everybody on this wall is dead," and she read a name slowly.

J.D. can't read, but he listened and said, "I *know* that, Grace. Look at this . . . what does this say?" and she read another name.

Shelley walked ahead of us because she's always a little embarrassed to be seen with her family, even though the people who saw her were never going to see her again. A man rushed over to where I was standing. He had an umbrella and a son with him.

"Is that the name, Daddy? Did you find him yet?"

"It said section J . . . let's see . . ." He ran his finger

down name after name. I started to cry, so I turned away. It's not that I was crying about that family. It was something else.

"Here he is! Susan? I found him!" the man called. A woman also carrying an umbrella came over to him.

"Yeah . . . there he is," she said. I turned to see her peering into the black shine of the wall.

"I knew we'd find him," the man said.

It wasn't the war, exactly, that was making me cry. I guess it was the sheer rage. I mean, there were all these guys on a wall—dead. Thousands and thousands of them . . . one of them, surely, could have been Mr. Right for me. And so I cried all the way back to the car because of all the men who died who could be alive to balance out some of this pain.

A woman at Fort Bragg is quoted in the paper as saying, "You gotta understand . . . my husband was born with a combat diaper on." And so her husband and sixty thousand other troops were sent over to Saudi Arabia last week. We here at home are afraid Saddam Hussein will use chemical weapons on them.

I dread the thought of war with Iraq for no other reason than we already have a horrible shortage of men. If we sail away another million there won't be any left for me even if I *do* lose thirty-five pounds. Kind of kills your incentive.

Elvira Dirge sent a message yesterday. "Hoping you recover. All our best." Now it is clear as daylight. She's crazy. I mean, I haven't been sick in years.

Sweet Vacation Pie ¤¤¤¤¤¤¤¤¤¤¤¤¤¤¤¤¤¤¤¤¤¤¤

1. *Station wagon or small van (Colt Vistas are the best for this)*
2. *Two or more children with coloring books and new boxes of crayons*
3. *Headphone sets so everybody can listen to his or her own music*
4. *Parent to drive vehicle and hold map and read instructions at the same time*

Fill car with above. Put on wrong road and melt over low flame. When completely dissolved and mixed up, add thunderstorm, late night, booked hotels everywhere, no reservations, and a dog that was given to the family en route somewhere in Wilmington, Delaware. Pour into pastry shell and bake until fork in center comes out chewed.

I wish now that I had held on to Rolando Skitchetti when I had him. Not that I *had* him, but he was interested and he worked for the garbage truck company. When we went on vacation it was two days before garbage pickup, so I left all the garbage on the front porch and locked the screen and figured it would smell but I could put it out when we got home from our trip. When we got home the raccoons had broken into the porch and strewn the garbage everywhere . . . it was horrible . . . and when we went into the house I realized slowly that nothing was as it should have been. At first I thought we had been robbed. But then I saw paw prints . . . through the broken glass and ruined food that was everywhere. That cute little raccoon family had moved in while we were gone and decimated the place.

"Have you had trouble receiving your Sunday paper?" the woman asks me on the phone.

"We don't get the paper," I say.

"You don't? Well, I'd like to tell you about our $2.29 special that's going on today and today only for those people who have not yet signed up to receive our Sunday paper . . . and if you'd like to get the weekly at this time there would only be an additional charge of . . ." I hang up. Five minutes later the phone rings again. It's either for Shelley or it's a creditor I'm guessing.

"Hello. Gabby Fulbriten?"

"Yes," I say cautiously.

"Gabby, you are the winner of our photo contest and we'd like to set up a time for you to receive your eight-by-ten matte finish at only $8.95. What would be a good time, seven fifteen or eight twenty?"

"Eight twenty," I say. It pops out before I realize what I've done.

"Now, Gabby, if you can list ten people for me over the phone who might want this fabulous winner's portrait, we'll give you an additional gift worth over seventy-five dollars. First start with your best friends . . ."

"Well," I say, pausing to think.

Simple Clutter Consommé ¤¤¤¤¤¤¤¤¤¤¤¤¤¤¤¤¤

1. *6 or 7 people a day calling you, offering gifts and bonus points if you will give them cash*
2. *Mailman arriving with 6 pieces of mail: 2 bills and 1 threatening letter from the Creditor's Marketplace in Honking, Ohio, and 3 letters confirming your name on the winners' list of 3 different nationwide contests (never enter contests; they enter you on their own)*
3. *A scary guy who keeps calling from somewhere in the world, asking you to call him back on his 800 number*

Sift ingredients thoroughly, looking for any particles of truth. Add to water that has been mixed with beef jelly. Cover and simmer over low heat, making sure nothing jells or is connected. Add to this people you wish were your friends, any letters you never get, any offers that you are still waiting for. Serve in bowls and garnish.

During our trip to Washington, I took the children to see where they make the money. It was jammed but we were the last people to get in, so we dallied in the back sometimes to see better as the group trooped by all squished into a fat line. Several beautiful black women were leading the tours and explaining what it was that we were staring at.

"Down here you will see, if you'll just lean this way, the presses are still going, they go at an incredible rate, never stopping, twenty-four hours a day." Her voice connected all the sentences together. She seemed never to breathe. J.D. watched with interest as huge sheets of twenty-dollar bills rolled out of the machine. A sign said, YOU THINK YOU FEEL BAD? I JUST PRINTED MY ENTIRE LIFE'S SALARY IN TEN MINUTES.

Another place we visited was the Washington Monument. It was easy to get to and there was parking around it, but I thought it was very boring. I mean, it seemed to just be a big *thing* shooting up toward the sky . . . just this *phallic* symbol building with a line of people around it like a loopy bracelet. They were all waiting to get inside, but I didn't want to get inside. It looked narrow and there wasn't a single window that I could see. I wasn't going to spend all day waiting to get in there to take a rickety elevator to the top. Shelley was furious because I wouldn't let her go up inside. I tried to explain that it wasn't very interesting and we would have more fun at the White

House. But she wanted to go inside the Washington Monument. Nothing would deter her. So instead of going happily off to the White House, we had a big fight and went back to our hotel in Baltimore.

I said, "Shelley, when you turn eighteen and you come to D.C. you can go in there all you want. But right now you aren't old enough to go without me and I'm not staying . . ."

Sometimes people seem like sheep to me. Why do they all crowd over to the Washington Monument to get inside? I mean, there's no priceless art, there's no gold-lined walls, there's no torture chambers or fascinating writing on the walls . . . it's just a *thing* that goes *up.* I have a theory that it's the parking lot that is the big draw there, but what do I know? I am so ignorant about our country's history sometimes . . . Maybe the Washington Monument is the burial ground for our presidents or something important like that. Maybe it was given to us by the Indians or the French or the Iranians, as a peace offering or a treaty. I mean, I should have at *least* stopped and read the brass plaque.

NAVAL OFFICER SEEKS SWEET BLONDE WHO IS WILLING TO BE LED. MUST BE QUIET TYPE, PETITE, GOOD COOK. SMALL FEET, WHITE TEETH, GOOD COMMUNICATIONS SKILLS.

I always wanted to be the girlfriend of a naval officer or a cop or something. Maybe its the pro-war feeling that's sweeping the country, but I'd love to fall in love with a guy in uniform and holsters. Or maybe it's that I'm cracking under the loneliness. The pressure on a single parent is horrendous, and when you are forced to celibacy your sense of awareness is not so keen as confused.

Hester and I took a walk last night. We traipsed down toward the lower cow pasture and back up and into the old dump, all the while my new dog running in circles around us. My new dog came about through a psychic experience (another thing that happens to single parents more often than happily married women). I was driving the kids through Baltimore when it struck me that I had to have a Hungarian sheepdog right then and there. I mean, I pulled the car over and made a phone call to a dog-grooming store I was so desperate for a Hungarian sheepdog. It was weird. The groomer didn't know what they were but she gave me the number of a Polish sheepdog breeder who tried for an hour to talk me into a Polish sheepdog (only $600). Finally she gave me the number in Pennsylvania of a puli breeder and I called.

"Wrong time of the year for puppies," she said. "Call me back in the spring, but as I have a waiting list of sixty people it probably won't be for two years. Did you want it sooner than that?"

"I really want one *now,*" I said, trying not to be desperate. "What I really want is an adult dog . . . you know, puppies chew too much stuff up . . . I guess it's hopeless . . . because I'm poor and couldn't afford to buy one . . ."

"Well," said the woman, "I do have a three-year-old male return you could have . . . *maybe.*"

Hester said she didn't get any cucumbers this year on account of a big woodchuck and a big rabbit. "They come into the yard together every night . . . I go in the house when I see 'em and I tell Fitch [her husband] and he gets the gun, but by the time he's out of the house they're gone. We've been trying all summer to get them," she explained to me. We were avoiding the new condos being built on the hill. I could just cry when I see the bulldozers plowing up the earth and knocking down the dead elms. The thing about those dead elms is, we have these pileated woodpeckers that love to peck on the dead trees and the blackbirds love to rest there in the spring. I hate to see them get bulldozed down to make a better view for the condos.

"They're ugly," Hester said of the trees, but I disagreed with her.

"They're beautiful," I said. "They are perfect for the birds to land on . . . they're strange looking and . . ." But what did it matter? They were coming down, and the new condos were going up faster than the last set. These condos are for poor people. They plan on letting "low-income" people rent these for about three hundred dollars a month. They call their prospective renters low-income instead of welfare recipients or poor people because *low income* sounds more ordinary. It's kind of unordinary for you to be poor . . . even though a lot of us are, we have to pretend that we aren't. It's like the photography guy said when we went in to get our 8 x 10 matte finish of Shelley for only $8.95 . . .

"For six hundred fifty dollars you can have her photograph embossed on wood [he held up a slab of wood] covered with sealable plastic so that even if the kids bite it [he took a bite of the wood] it won't spoil the finish. Now if you have a MasterCard, by all means put it on that and just pay twenty dollars a month. Isn't that cheap? Twenty dollars a month for eight of these wood photographs of your daughter? Now, who do you want to get the first three? Come on . . . Grandma? Grandpa? Mom? Dad?"

Shelley was disgusted with the guy. "God, they're ugly," she blurted out. I laughed.

"Teenagers," I said.

"And I don't have a Grandpa," she said. "He's dead. I *hate* these pictures, Mom."

"We call them photographs," the man corrected. "Now for only three hundred dollars you can have two embossed on wood with the ultra finish and three just in solid brass frames. Does that sound more like *you*?"

"I can't afford that," I said.

"What? Twenty dollars a month? You can't afford twenty dollars a month? Come on!"

"But it isn't the twenty dollars a month," I said. "It's six hundred dollars. Having it on MasterCard doesn't make it free . . . it just puts it off . . . and anyway, I don't have MasterCard." Not having MasterCard always shocks these people.

"I see," he said, packing up his wood slabs and putting the color prints into an envelope.

"I'm poor," I said.

"I see," he said again, even more shocked. "Well, hey, I don't get rich doing this but I have more fun than I do suckin' on limes."

I smiled at him and Shelley glared at him and we left, hearing him usher an unattractive couple into his back room.

"You're going to love these," he was saying. "The air brush gives it that extra special professional . . ."

Words of Wisdom from the Bible

Back on a diet, that's the way it goes. This time I tell myself I will lose that thirty pounds, which have mysteriously turned into forty-five. Sometimes when I am searching for someone to make the decisions for me (when there's no guy around you have to do all the deciding on your own) I will open the Bible to any page and hold my finger in one place and take whatever it says as a sign. Today I read this while I munched on the five-ounce apple allotted to me on the Diet Center program:

> AND JESUS SAID INTO THEM, can the children of the bridechamber fast while the bridegroom is with them? So long as they have the bridegroom with them, they cannot fast.
>
> But the days will come, when the bridegroom shall be taken away from them, and they shall fast in those days.
>
> —Mark 2:19, 20

Am I psychic or is God speaking to me? I mean, here I have been so fat for so long and now the bridegroom is *really* gone and I'm on a diet. I think it's a sign that *this* time I can really lose the weight and keep it off.

(And no man putteth new wine into old bottles) so if I want a new man and a new relationship then I have to get myself a new bottle . . . I have to lose forty-five pounds. That's insurmountable if I see it as a chunk figure . . . but half a pound a day seems easy enough.

Then, since that question worked so well, I asked the Bible if I would find true love with a man on Earth, and I put my finger on Isaiah:

> BABYLON AND CHALDEA SHALL be destroyed for their iniquities. None shall save

them [chapter 47]. Come down and sit in the dust, virgin daughter of Babylon, sit on the ground . . . for thou shalt no more be called tender and delicate.

Probably what that means is that I shouldn't ask the Bible Ouija board sorts of questions. God doesn't want me playing tarot cards with his wisdom. So I apologize. And I hope that what was in store for Chaldea is not my fate. Whoever she was, she must have really irritated the people.

Things I Learned to Do from TV About the Earth

1. Pull or cut apart plastic six-pack can holders so the whales won't choke or something on them.

2. Wash and remove all labeling from cat food and dog food cans and from the jumbo olive cans and put it in the blue box outside by the road. The recycling truck comes once a week and takes it away to somewhere.

3. Ask for paper bags in the store if you forgot your canvas bags and when you get home, cut out the bags to be book covers for your teenager.

4. Take a real cup with you when you go to the bakery for fresh coffee. Never use those Styrofoam ones. Always complain about them when you drive through McDonald's.

5. Don't leave the water running when you brush

your teeth. Never forget that we have about twenty years left before the whole planet becomes a filthy hot box with poisoned water and everybody getting cancer.

6. Get a VCR to keep you from thinking. Anxiety should permeate your every pore and you should need sleeping pills at night to keep from dreaming of the end of the world. Lose hope, regain hope. Lose hope, find a ray of hope. Lose hope. Plunge ahead. Lose hope, regain hope.

> DWW SEEKS DWM OR DBM TO SHARE IN LOVE AND HOPE. ARE YOU OUT THERE? WHAT IS OUT THERE? PHOTO A PLUS. CANDLELIGHT AND QUIET WALKS AWAIT YOU.

Yesterday I went to see the Dalai Lama, his Holiness from Tibet. I went with a friend and we arrived two hours early, but it was like we were waiting in line for the Beatles. Cars were parking on huge grassy fields, people were walking together toward one place with one goal in mind . . . to feel better, to have hope. They drifted toward the entrance of the hockey rink like years ago we had drifted toward Woodstock. My friend and I found a seat halfway back. I ran into the sister of my first love who, I guess, got all messed up since I knew him. So the three of us, all women, sat together. I counted the women in the rows I could see, and there would be fifteen women, three men; seventeen women, four men. There was not one row that I could see that had more men than women or even came close to being equal. The few men were coveted and many women circled around them, chatting and smiling continually. Women are taught that men don't like gloomy girls, so all women smile and smile around men.

This sweet, small bald man in red and yellow robes came down the sideline. Everyone was bowing to him and staring . . . we all thought he was the Dalai Lama.

"That's him," my friend whispered. Then she said, "Well, maybe it isn't . . . He looks smaller than in the pictures."

"They always make them look bigger in the publicity shots," I said.

We decided it was him, but then the room became hushed and policemen came down the aisle backward, with the Dalai Lama following, bowing and praying and smiling—ever smiling, like the women who so desperately want a man smile. Hope and kindness were in his smile. We were all very excited. I decided then that maybe my life was about to change. Maybe I would really hear the answer and really find the right understanding of the world.

He went to the stage at the front. The president of the college spoke for about ten boring minutes and then the Dalai Lama, who was constantly referred to as "His Holiness," began to teach. I strained to see him. He was hidden to me by hundreds and hundreds of dark suits and heads and shoulders . . .

And his interpreter spoke in obscure phrases: ". . . the inner self and the inner light and the inner something-or-other . . ." and then the sound system was faltering and failing. Actually, I couldn't understand anything. I couldn't even tell when His Holiness spoke in English or in Tibetan. I couldn't see his kind face or his gesturing arms . . . I knew he was speaking of our dying Earth . . . of mother's milk (I caught that) . . . of *family* . . . He sounded like a sound guy . . . a man who understood . . . but nobody could hear him. The crowd grew restless . . . they had come to be saved . . . like Jesus on the hill . . . like Moses on the mountain, like Joseph Smith on the Hill Comorah, they wanted to hear the absolute truth . . . the reason for their suffering.

One crippled guy even had stopped His Holiness when he was walking toward the stage and had gestured to his ruined legs, and the Dalai Lama smiled and agreed and moved on. He was not Jesus. He was full of love and understanding, but who could possibly answer to this terrible mess we humans are in? Even God is silent. We are alone, and I guess if we don't band together we will flounder, leaderless sheep that we are, and die in smoldering radiation or gassy greenhouse air.

When I left I could have cried. My old love's sister and I stood by our cars and watched an Indian group eat lunch. They opened the trunk of their Mercedes-Benz and lifted the lids off elegant casserole dishes. The women in saris hurried here and there with plates and silverware and served men in business suits before serving themselves.

"I wish I was like that," I said, wishing I could cook and bring an elegant lunch in a fancy car and serve some wonderful man in a suit, all the while being wrapped in lovely thin material.

"They don't even look cold," my first love's sister said.

"No . . . see, that one is shivering . . . she's just covering up how she really feels," I said.

"Well, I better go . . . I don't know if I'll come back to see him tomorrow during the meditation group."

I hugged her. She looks just like her brother. "Please send him my love," I said, meaning her brother.

"Yeah, okay," she said, but probably she would forget. A lot of people are forgetful these days, which I attribute to Chernobyl. Radiation seeping into everything . . .

I don't mean to be disrespectful about His Holiness, I don't mean that he was not the real thing or anything like that . . . I just felt awful for all those people who congregated to wrest a grain of hope out of our difficult world. When my sister decided to take a job in Morocco and flew off today, I asked her husband what he thought . . . "Do you think it's safe? I mean, Saddam Hussein and all?"

He was quiet for a minute over the phone. "It's safer than New York," he finally said.

When my father first died, there were the four of us—Mother, my oldest sister, Nina, and me. My oldest sister had a stream of boyfriends coming and going . . . When she wasn't crying with my mother over Daddy, she was dressing up in leather coats and going off with Harvard boys whom she called things like "Prince" and "Buffalo." Mother was rather useless at that point, soon after Daddy died . . . so my oldest sister, Jean, became the surrogate parent for a while, only she was way too tough on us. Nina and I got our hair washed and our fingernails clipped down to the quick by our oldest sister while Mother feebly tried to rally. But several years after Daddy died, Jean moved away with her future husband to another country. Still, Nina and I remember the nights she used to stay up late with a boyfriend making patience . . . a fudgelike caramel dessert. When it was all cooked she poured it into a buttered plate and it hardened into a big round candy. Nina and I always stood in the kitchen doorway begging for a piece, but Jean said, "Wait till tomorrow . . . have patience . . . go to bed," then she would turn back to her boyfriend, "Here, Buffalo," we could hear her say as we climbed the stairs to bed, "have a piece!"

In the morning, the plate was always empty.

Just Desserts ¤¤¤¤¤¤¤¤¤¤¤¤¤¤¤¤¤¤¤¤¤¤¤¤¤¤¤¤

1. Cowman removes babies from field. Mothers bellow long into the night. All day they moo and rush from one end of the front field to the other. The cowman does not answer his phone. The mother cows do not give up. They are relentless in their search for their children.

2. The dog is sixteen years old. The vet diagnoses cancer in throat and breast. She wheezes and coughs and pees on the floor. I cancel the euthanasia appointment four times . . . give up and dissolve beside her on the floor in a helpless pool of tears. Dog rallies, seems less breathless.

3. In the middle of the night a foster child I once helped calls and sobs from somewhere in Ohio that her mother is hurting her . . . that her mother is drunk again; that her mother is leaving her alone again to drink at the bar. Her sobbing reaches into my nightmares and calls up the worst childhood terrors. "It's *not* your fault," I say into the mouthpiece. Foster child says, "I better hang up . . . I have to go to school in the morning. I'll be all right . . . the door is locked . . ."

4. In my dreams I am trying to love an Indian boy-man. He likes me. My mother intervenes and ruins it.

Pills lie all over the car floor. I am screaming because my mother won't let me love men . . . won't let men love me. Mother Earth.

5. I hit my son with a shoe three times for hitting his sister while I was upstairs. In my mind I hear the Dalai Lama saying, "See the point from different views. Keep peace in the family. Maintain compassion, understanding."

Blend in the pain until you are unable to escape it. Fold in the sound of agony. Stir just enough to moisten. Guilt and sorrow should be light in color. Bake into your own bones. Shrinking from sides will occur . . . serve to everyone gathered at the mountain, even Jesus if he is there.

Not long ago a member of the Mormon Church stopped by my house. It was the farm family from outside of Leadbelly. They always sat in the back pews because they arrived late for sacrament meetings. "They can't come till they do morning chores," someone had whispered to me . . . but even though I am inactive, members still stop by, hoping to bring me back toward salvation. So the farm family stopped in after church; it was fast and testimony Sunday and their children looked hungry and I knew the mother wasn't drinking water because her mouth looked dry. I didn't ask them in. Grace and J.D. were boiling hot dogs on the stove and I had a pot of coffee on the counter . . . so we stood in the front yard. "We wanted to see how you were doing," the mother of the group said. "We were just leaving church and we decided to see how you were . . . we sure do miss you at church . . ." Mormons are a blunt people. They come right to the point and then stare at you with big round eyes or little squinty eyes and you have to respond . . . they leave you no choice. "Well, . . . thank you . . ."

"Is there anything I could do to help you come back to church? We could pick you up on Sundays if you'd like . . . it's no problem. We can swing by around nine forty-five . . . ?"

I looked at the ground. "We have several new brethren," she said. "There's a gentleman from New York State who comes to our branch . . . and an older man who has just joined. In fact, his baptism was last Sunday. You see how much you're missing?" She smiled at me. I looked at her van full of Latter-day kids. Her husband was standing near my lilac bush looking uncomfortable in his Sunday clothes. They were so united. They were sure of everything before them . . . chores, home-cooked meals, scripture reading in the evenings, church on Sundays, no infidelity, no divorce, no matter what . . . sealed together for time and all eternity according to Iggy's explanation of the Mormon marriage. "It's worth a try," she said, moving closer to me. She kept her shining eyes on my face, even when I wouldn't look, she shined her eyes on me.

"New brethren?" I said after a moment.

She smiled, encouraging me. "Two new brethren in our branch! And we have a sister who moved out from Utah this spring. She is a wonderful gardener and she has been showing the other sisters how to improve our food storage." The farm mother was beaming her face around my yard now, smiling at everything. By saying one word in response I had stepped into that space of unsurety . . . I had SAVABLE written on my forehead. "Yes, and she is working at the green grocers . . . isn't that where you used to work?"

Slip and Go Down (Savable Soul Soup) ¤¤¤¤¤¤¤

1. Somebody to come up with a new idea
2. A bunch of people to follow the rules
3. A list of righteous rules
4. An iron rod

To make Slip and Go Down, add the new idea to the righteous rules and the bunch of righteous people. When the people begin to separate, some will rise to the top and others will sink. Stir constantly so sinkers don't stick together. Add iron rod to grasp on to and after a certain unspecified amount of time, remove rod without warning. What is left in the pot is Slip and Go Down. What clings to the iron rod is Savable Soul Soup. Refrigerate Savable Soul Soup and repeat process. Discard Slip and Go Down.

The word "brethren" implies in itself a warm man in a raccoon coat . . . at least in my mind it does. It reminds me of the guy in McCabe and Mrs. Miller who loves the whore and wants to marry her but she is an opium addict and goes off with some Chinese people in the end. The guy in that wore a raccoon coat and looked like the word "brethren." In the Mormon Church, though, it means "men." Plain and simple. Men who followed Joseph Smith to Illinois and then Brigham Young to Salt Lake and built cities and temples and had children by the hundreds . . . wives and children and prayers all contained in their handcarts . . . those deeply religious men who labored with their large useful hands to build the Mormon dreams on Earth in order to attain celestial glory. Those brethren who traveled west with slender obedient wives (myself not among them) who went on to have daughters who grew up knowing they would marry and make pretty things in relief society (again I wasn't there) and who pioneered the East Coast later, like where Leadbelly is now, brethren and sisters and babies all warm and breathy like homemade soup in fall. Just the clockwork of it is enough to lure me. The obvious, predictable outcome . . .

Of course that, and knowing my testimony is still in there somewhere. The burning realization that *this is what we are here to do.* Band together and make ourselves one enormous family, Earthwide, all cities and countries and hamlets as brothers and sisters on our planet. Get together and clean up our room before Mom and Dad get home because they are going to be ripped when they see what we've done to the house.

My Mormon side gets the better of me . . . Amen.

During the winter months we oft recall that delicious thin soup our mother or aunt made . . . with perhaps a little soggy celery in it or onion slivers but mostly the flavor of a guardian. Easy to duplicate, but hard to capture in entirety, named aptly. . . .

Blessed Broth ########################

1. *Broth—made by adding salt, carrots, Italian tomatoes, and assorted meats such as beef, lamb and chicken cooked in pot and in enough water to cover, draining the broth and then discarding the stewed matter*
2. *Stalks of celery, sliced Zen style*
3. *Onion, chopped*
4. *Clove of garlic, chopped*
5. *Warm bowls, cloth napkins, conversation with a child*

Combine first 4 ingredients and boil till celery is soft. Pour into warm bowls and converse.

The cows have finally quit crying. Today is the first time since Mr. Boots took away their babies that I have not gotten up to the sound of wailing bovines. Mr. Boots stopped by yesterday in his pickup truck to visit them. He brought them hay and apples and spent an hour or more scratching their heads and feeding them. They circled around him and mooed their sorrows. He was right in amongst them as he always is when he visits, and later he said he saw the pain in their eyes. He stopped to chat with me as he was leaving, and he said, "Boy, I know they were sad . . . I saw it in their eyes. You could see it . . . believe me, their babies are just the same. I've got them down't the house, and they don't even stay in the fence. They walk right through it. These girls would too if they saw their babies out here in the road. Nuthin'd stop them if they saw them babies, believe me."

"Mr. Boots, why can't you leave them together?" I said. I had been really upset at first, but when the mooing subsided over the course of some days I had gotten used to the sadness. Still . . .

"I mean, couldn't they just be together?"

"These babies here would starve the little ones inside 'em. When they were born they wouldn't get enough milk. Then the littler ones'd die, see . . ."

"These mothers are pregnant?" I said.

"Oh, yeah," he said. Mr. Boots seems so innocent. Sitting there in his pickup truck with some children with him, smiling after feeding his cows apples.

"Molly's already down't the house gettin' ready to

have hers." All Mr. Boots's cows have names. Molly and Mellow and Shoo-Fly and Prancer. Their names are stapled into their ears on plastic cards. Sometimes I think I will give up eating meat for love of Mellow and Annie, but then I find myself at McDonald's and I'm ordering a hamburger and fries and I can hardly recall the look of anguish I read in the eyes of this little herd.

"Them babies were bellerin' bad. I can imagine how these here were. Next time," Mr. Boots continues, "I'll have ta lock 'em up in the lower pasture. Then you won't hear 'em."

"I wish you'd just quit doing it," I said, but I smiled at him when I said it, because of course it would be rude to say it and not just be joking.

COW PIE ¤¤¤¤¤¤¤¤¤¤¤¤¤¤¤¤¤¤¤¤¤¤¤¤¤¤¤¤¤¤¤

1. *1 herd large milk cows*
2. *Accompanying calves*
3. *Fields of wild asters, wild miniature daisies, Queen Anne's lace*
4. *Empathetic-but-goes-ahead-anyway cowman*
5. *A single woman watching from her window*

Put herd of mothers and calves in field of flowers. Let stand until daisies are eaten and they are enveloped in Queen Anne's lace like a painting of childhood, of innocence, of brown-eyed trust. Stir in cowman, pickup trucks, ropes, electric fencing. Lure with salt licks. Once scene has congealed, set woman on window duty, to watch and weep for the wordless cattle. Woman should be spokesperson for the group, a firm crust on top but concealing a gelatinous center. Refrigerate until tolerable.

A car drove by me today with a bumper sticker saying DON'T KNOW, DON'T CARE. It set me to longing. How I wish I could say that!

Fall is setting in. The nights are very cold and during the day the weather rocks from flat to blustery. The leaves are beginning to rattle. Hester can't walk in the evenings because she is busy canning tomatoes. Her cucumbers went kaput this year . . . maybe due to the raccoons. Fall is comforting. I have been getting in my wood and cleaning out the house until only necessary stuff remains—to leave room for snowsuits and boots and piles of wood. Hester is filling her larder with pickles and tomato sauces and ripe pumpkins. I am dieting and considering when to put the dog to sleep . . . the children love the crispness in the air. Grace says the air tastes like snow. Of course, it never snows much anymore because of the change in the global weather, but it's exciting nonetheless to be ready for a giant snowfall . . . like when I was little and the snow fell until it covered the windows and we had to wear snowshoes across the crispy top. We had sleds with runners on them that raced across the top of the deep snow. We had to dig out our car every morning. Now I don't even have to shovel the driveway. It never snows enough to cover anything. But we are getting prepared. It is in the preparing that the fun is generated. When I start the fire in the morning to take the chill out of the kitchen, I long for a boyfriend. Wouldn't it be wonderful to have a man stomp into the kitchen with an armload of wood, requesting a biscuit hot from the oven? Maybe it's just the biscuit hot from the oven that I'm longing for . . . dieting always confuses me. I see winter as a long series of hot food. Stew on the wood cookstove. Hot bread in the oven. Cookies on shiny sheets of tin. Eggnog and whiskey in the cold evening air with a friend . . . This digression is probably due to snacktime. I need my rye Vita Crisp and quarter of an apple with a frosty glass of water.

I received a long letter from Iggy Stains last week. He broke down and asked me to marry him. He said he had always loved me, since the day I opened the door and he had entered my house as a Mormon missionary, but of course then it wouldn't have been appropriate to mention it. He urged me to write back and tell him yes or no . . . He wondered if my children would mind that he was younger than me . . .

Dear Iggy:

YES! Yes, I will marry you and come to live with you on base. I will wash your combat clothes and shine your black boots in the evenings by the light of the color TV. I will be a military wife, wave bravely as you fly off to Saudi Arabia. I will train the children to respect you and I'll keep our little bungalow clean. I'll vacuum the orange-brown carpet every day and we will attend church on Sundays from 9 to 1. YES, Iggy Stains, I will marry you! I will go to homemaking night at the church with the other wives, carrying my Jell-O salad mold and my needlework. In the mornings, Iggy, we will have Kool-Aid instead of coffee because we will be Mormons who do not break the words of wisdom. I will smile all the time to show you I am cheery (men don't like gloomy women!!) AND I will say yes to everything you suggest. Yes, Iggy, I will be Mrs. Stains.

From an admirer on the East Coast,
Gabby Fulbriten

If only I could answer him! But his letter, so innocently put, lies sadly on the bathroom floor. I see it every morning as I head toward the coffee downstairs, and I feel a pang of regret . . . of sorrow . . . but I cannot bring myself to pick it up. What if he gets called away to Saudi Arabia before I let him know what I feel? What if his plane is gunned down by Saddam

Hussein's crazy Iraqis? What *do* I feel? Do I even *like* Iggy?

Dear Gabby:
Though our paths do not always meet, we are hoping you have a safe journey.
From your friend, Ms. E. Dirge

Exhausted. The sun is going down and I am staggering outside to see the ocean before it is too late. All day I have been checking in a grocery store and helping to put back together the books that were mixed up . . . but not in my town where I longed to meet the grocery-chain representative. No. I was called away to Maine by a woman who knew I did fine work when it comes to repairing poor books and redoing some of the bookkeeping altogether, as well as dubbing in some checking time. They paid my way here, to an island in Maine, and after working all day I planned to go look at the ocean.

I'm so tired. I can hardly watch the last of the lobster boats disappearing from my view. At lunch, some of the girls from the Fun Feed took me up a mountain to a teahouse and we had popovers in the wind outside, looking down on a beautiful lake. I keep waiting to hear that famous Maine accent, but so far all the people I've met are southern and have the Georgia drawl. They tell me Maine people are losing their accents. "There's a leveling out going on," one woman tells me. That makes me miss Hester. She is not all leveled out. She is a full-fledged Vermonter, with a warm accent and a knack for gardening. Anyway, I feel weird here. This place is in the deep woods . . . there are pine trees surrounding me in this camp on the ocean. They tell me there are rednecks here, but I haven't seen anyone. Also, trying to stick to the Diet Center program, with no stores around here, I have eaten fourteen apples today. Plus those two buttered popovers. No leveling off with me. But is there a leveling off in humans? Are we all turning into the same person?

I can't help but feel heartbroken. I took a walk this evening on this island in Maine, along the shore of the ocean. Round rocks, smooth from the years of tide washing them, were lumpy under my worn-out sneakers. I guess I needn't describe my sneakers, but the fact is my poverty follows me, even to Maine, where the sky is old-fashioned and heavenly. Like the photos of a sky in heaven. The sky of the celestial kingdom. And I walked to the foamy water's edge in my slipshod sneakers and I could feel the battered Earth speaking to me. I could feel the sorrow, the broken heart of the Earth crying up through my sneakers . . . maybe because they had holes in them, I could feel the Earth drawing the tears out of my own eyes to weep for her. It was uncontrollable. Not a gush of sobbing but a wail and a stream of salt tears into the salt ocean for the salt of the Earth.

Coq au Fear ¤¤¤¤¤¤¤¤¤¤¤¤¤¤¤¤¤¤¤¤¤¤¤¤¤¤

1. A cabin (owned, oddly enough, by a famous catering chef)
2. A forest of pines and birch and heavy dark ferns; silence
3. A sound under the kitchen sink. Squirrel? Rats? Creaking somewhere
4. The ocean, rolling in and out in the dark. The dark comes instantly, obliterating
5. Realization that the fear follows you. From Vermont to Maine. From your bedroom to a dark road . . . inescapable

Frightened chicken should be cooked till meat falls from the bone. Gnaw the bone and place meat under the stars. Sky should be crowded with constellations. The bigger the sky, the more lonely that which is beneath it. Coq au Fear should not be served; it should be thrust upon one. Compatible plate companions: Horror Tostadas, Just Desserts. If an aperitif is called for, a dry red wine . . . or Kool-Aid if you're serving Mormons.

I just read my Bazooka bubblegum fortune: START A BAKERY IF YOU'VE GOT THE DOUGH. And what's more, Julia Child was spotted in the grocery store today while I was working out in the back room. Those books were a mess, but that's not the point. If

I'd been checking at the time, I would have asked her how she finds those wild mushrooms . . . and how come she isn't a total *blimp* from cooking all that fabulous food? I seem to be veering off into food talk again. I can sense that I'm ready for my fifteenth apple.

Today, after Fun Feed let me off work, I went down to the ocean again for a walk along the rocky beach. Do they bring in those round rocks to make a shore or do they just arrive there on their own? Anyway, I found a huge boulder out aways into the water and I sat on it and closed my eyes. The tide pounded in and pulled back, in and pull back, again and again and again, like a dedicated worker mopping a bus station floor . . . back and forth and back and forth. I could feel the tide as a living, aware substance, doing its job without question, back and forth, for a very specific reason. Not stopping to wonder but just going forward, again and again. My eyes were closed and I could feel that water like it was speaking to me. I almost fell off the rock too. But I don't know . . . maybe I'm really losing it this time. I mean, I can feel the Earth crying up through my sneakers and I can feel the tidewater like it's really alive, almost like it could speak but has nothing to say . . .

"Jus' doin' my job," it might say, "jus' doin' my job."

I drove through a huge forest park after work to try to calm down . . . apparently Julia Child breezed through again and I missed her. *Again.* But today I did hear a couple of Maine accents. They are lovely sounding. Vermont with a twang of the South, or something. In this forest I went driving through, I came upon a sign that said FREE. PICK YOUR OWN, FREE, so I stopped and pulled off to the side a little and got out, holding my coffee cup, ready to pick it for free, whatever it was. And there was before me meadow after meadow of blueberries . . . just like *Blueberries for Sal* looked in the pictures . . . remember that children's book? Well, there were fields and mountains all covered with blueberries, right there where I stood. So I filled my cup, and I didn't eat many, because I thought if I filled my cup without eating any, my children would be happy staying with my sister in Vermont. Do you ever do that? If I do this fast enough, nothing bad will happen? Or if I count to twenty before the phone rings, then so-and-so will fall in love with me? It's possible that I'm going mad. All this driving and then constantly, constantly, I am trying to understand the human dilemma. I mean, can't I just give it a rest?

No. No. Because today a girl said to me, "I can't stop crying about my parents' divorce. Don't mind me . . . I always cry. I can't stop. My dad . . . doesn't understand . . . that my mom just needed a change . . . and my little sister is *so* angry. She won't show her feelings." The girl had tears pouring down her face while she told me this. I was bagging her groceries and listening, and she was looking away the whole time. It came about because I told her I was a single mother and I missed my kids. And it turns out she is only fourteen, shopping for her mother . . . just a child who carries all the weight of a divorce on her shoulders.

"It's my sister I worry about," she said, but she wouldn't look at me.

"Well," I said, touching her arm sympathetically, "you can still love your dad . . . even if you aren't living with him anymore."

She smiled then, and without looking at me, said, "But he says terrible things about my mother . . . He used to be so idealistic. He used to love her. And now, I don't know. They hate each other. But my dad, he won't talk about it."

"Did you say you wanted a freezer bag for this?" I asked, holding up the ice cream.

"I don't care," she said. So I put it in the paper bag loose, because the less plastic you use, the better off the whales will be. I looked for plastic along the beach, by the way, but happily found none. And while I was out on that boulder communing with the water, I reached in my finger and tasted the water. It was so salty. It was like drinking salt. It just amazed me. I was wondering why people stuck on rafts died of thirst . . . couldn't they drink the salty water? I mean, doesn't salt help you *retain* water? After I tasted it two times I felt sort of sick. Then I got afraid, remembering how AIDS blood and dirty needles get dumped in the water off certain coasts. I was afraid maybe I'd swallowed barnacle eggs and the barnacles would grow in my stomach.

Hester said tonight on our walk that the new low-income condominiums would be finished by the new year.

"They've been working round the clock to get the cement laid . . . you know, for the cellar holes . . . or the pad, rather. They don't have any cellars, far as I can see."

"I can't believe anybody can live in such a small space," I said, referring to the model condo we had peeked into the night before.

"I know it," she said. "How's your little dog doin'?"

"Not too good. I called the vet again this morning to have him come put her to sleep . . . you know, that guy with the traveling euthanasia van?"

"I've heard of him," Hester said.

"He said he'd do it. But he thought I should wait until she quits eating. That might take forever. She'll eat no matter what." I sounded like a heel to myself, but after all, these were facts. My dog really loves to eat. She's dying and she's sixteen and she can hardly open her mouth but she still slides the food in one side, even steals the cat food. So I can't imagine her giving up food.

"Anyway, I haven't got a hole dug for her. I can't dig six feet by myself. I need a man to help me for a day or two." This sounded like a good idea to me after I had said it. Hire a man for a few days, take it easy, look normal.

"Six feet? You don't need no six feet. Why, you can dig a place about so high," she said, holding her hands mildly apart. "I know Guy took and had his dog operated on last year, and he paid a fortune for it. He said later if he'd known now what he didn't know then, why, he'd a'taken it out back and shot it in the first place . . ."

"People really get attached to their animals," I said, sympathizing with Guy.

" 'Cause the poor little thing died anaways," Hester said, moving along quickly on the grassy path. "And you know they took Nuggets to that vet of yours," Hester said. She was pointing to my other neighbor's house.

"Nuggets?" I said.

"Hey-yup. Nuggets. They took Nuggets to that vet you had before and he charged them . . . oh, my gosh . . . he really charged them."

"He has a swimming pool," I said, and Hester nodded.

"I bet he does," she went on. "But they took Nuggets there and he said they had to have all that poor little dog's teeth pulled . . . can you imagine? A dog with no teeth? So they did. They had all Nuggets's teeth pulled. Cost them an arm and a leg. And then he had to be put to sleep anyways."

"My god," I said.

"Hey-yup. But can you believe that? A dog with no teeth?" She was laughing now. We were both laughing. We had circled up near where the mother cows were in the upper pasture and had followed the pathway back to my house.

"Look at that light," I said, pointing to the horizon of the sky. "Is that the moon coming up?"

"Could be the moon," Hester answered me. "Either that or the cheese factory."

My new dog was jumping all around us and running back and forth up and down the road because it was night and he gets fed at night. Everything loves to eat, I think. Sometimes I just sit at the kitchen table and read magazines on food . . . country lifestyle magazines that are full of warm pine kitchens and big harvest tables laden with breads and muffins and glazed items in heaps on platters. It's everything I ever needed in one photograph. A cozy, central, clean, checkered, frosted, missing ingredient. If I could just get *that* down my throat.

"Well, good night," I called to Hester. She was hurrying home.

" 'Night," she called back.

More Walking

Last night Hester and I took our usual walk. I was still in my apron because ever since joining a diet program I have been driven by some internal force to bake. I had just finished baking pumpkin-shaped sugar cookies and Grace was frosting them with orange icing. Geese flew over our heads as we perused the old town dump, looking for good wood. That's one of our missions on our walks. We check out the new condos being built and we go to the dump to look for good wood. Not that we gather any of it or come back later with a chain saw. We just notice that it's there.

"There's some birch," I said, pointing to a pile of felled trees.

"I know," Hester said, "and over there looks like some popple. Good wood too. I can't see why those poor people don't use this wood instead of goin' on welfare." I didn't respond to this. I think she knows I tend to side with the poor people . . .

"There go some ducks," I went on. "I hate duck-hunting season. I don't even like the taste of duck."

"I just take and parboil it," she said. "Then I put it in sodey and either fry it up or boil it till it's done."

One lone duck circled over the river below us.

"They mate for life," I said. I was feeling gloomy.

Winter is setting in and yet the weather remains rather warm. I worry about the greenhouse effect.

"There's some over there . . . looks like it could be maple. Is it?"

"Could be," Hester answered. We were turning around now and heading back.

"Wanna go look at how far they've gotten?" she asked, meaning the new condo site. I said no, I was tired and wanted to get back to my baking. I had in mind to make an apple crisp and maybe a pumpkin pie.

Mouthwatering Chapter

I lost twenty pounds at the Diet Center in a mere six weeks! Yes, thanks to Sybil, who founded it (I hear through the grapevine that she is a Mormon and that is why alcohol and coffee are discouraged on the program). Thanks to Sybil's wonderful idea, I have shrunk some. I feel better about myself. I don't lie in bed and eat chocolate kisses or dart from store to store buying pints of Ben & Jerry's ice cream. I no longer wait with the Volvos in the long line beside McDonald's drive-through window, twelve dollars in hand, ready to purchase and consume fries, McSandwiches and sundaes before I've even had the chance to pull back out into traffic. Now, as a member of the Diet Center program I eat a bran muffin or its equivalent for breakfast, an apple for snack, a salad for lunch, and a strip of chicken breast for dinner, topped off with some French green beans and followed at 7 P.M.

by another apple. I drink lots of healthy fresh water and steer away from soft drinks. And in the evening, for my daily exercise, I take a walk with Hester, who is just as eager to talk about food as I am.

Tonight we talk pies.

"Did you make that recipe in the *Buyer's Guide*?" she asks me as we stand around in the road after our walk, talking. We have already been up on the hill and seen the devastation done by the bulldozers, making tiny homes for our town's resident low-income people. The condos are all bunched together in a pine forest and we worry that they will saw down the trees for fear the low-income people will get hurt around them. Asphalt and blacktop are so much safer and easier to care for . . .

The trees look confused, scattered here and there around the ugly new buildings, and Hester and I quickly get depressed thinking about the hordes of new people due to arrive in a few months. Will there be fights at the old town dump? Will people beat their kids? Will the low-income people seem as faceless as the high-income people in the condos next to them?

"No, I didn't see that recipe," I say to Hester, back to the *Buyer's Guide*.

"Oh. I made it and it was good!" she says, and a smile crosses her face. She is all bundled up tonight against the cold wind that has been whipping through our street this evening. My cosmos are bending in the cold wind.

"Mmmhmmmm," she says. "Fitch doesn't often care for anything made with apple, but he ate a little of this. He likes blueberry."

We have found a subject we both like. Food. It takes our minds off the sad state of affairs on the ridge where all the building goes on all day long. Hester has to listen to it more than me . . . I'm closer to the old dump and don't get the traffic, like she does, of huge cement trucks throwing dust in her dooryard all day.

"It was called Apple Goody. Hey-yup. Boy, it was good . . . Now let me see . . . what did I put in it? Well, you layer your apples . . ." She tells me, and I insert it here.

Apple Goody

As told to me by Hester in the evening in the road.

Layer 4 cups apple in bottom of casserole dish.

Sprinkle with brown sugar, cinnamon, etc.

Then you take and mix your flour with your white sugar [the one in the paper called for too much sugar. We don't care for a goody that's too sweet. So about 1/2 cup sugar] and some butter [she melted hers but she thinks it" might be better if you don't melt it first]. Put the butter on the apples and add some oatmeal to your topping mixture and a little soda, just about 1/2 teaspoon, and then you put all that on the apples and put your casserole dish top on it ["A lid?" I say. She says, "Yes, that's what makes it so good"] and bake the whole thing till it's done. And boy, you have a little a that with some vanilla ice cream and mmmhmmm, it's chewy and so good.

"I've been wanting a pumpkin pie," I tell her after she finishes with her recipe. "A pumpkin pie with whipped cream . . ."

"Oh, so haven't I," she says, and we shift a little bit in the road, our adrenaline going up, this taboo subject of desserts and no one to hear us in the quiet dark of our street. "I like to make it with fresh pumpkin from the garden . . . trouble is, the raccoons have been eating everything every year, so we never get pumpkins . . ."

"I like ice cream on apple pie and whipped cream on pumpkin."

"That's what I had this mornin' for breakfast. A little Apple Goody with some whipped cream. My daughter called me last night, I forgot to tell you, and gave me an awful good recipe for soup. I had that this noontime. You just add your tomato and your onion and peppers and no salt, I didn't hear her say no salt, but some garlic, and I used canned tomatoes. And you cook that, and boy, I didn't have but a little bowl of it but it filled me right up. She's losing weight on it, and it does give you a full feeling. Oh, and I crumbled up some crackers in mine."

The leaves are all falling. Hester and I have

watched the rains and the winds knock down all the leaves and every day the colors on the mountains grow duller. The leaf peepers have all but disappeared from the state. Yet we stay on. In this place that has its hold on us, for whatever reasons, we remain. After all the out-of-staters and vacationers and leaves have left, here we are, looking up at a quarter moon and watching Canadian geese fly by.

I say the trouble with losing weight is that you can't stop thinking about it. I have been changing my clothes in front of the mirror for several hours, happily, black skirt on, flowered skirt, leotard . . . black skirt, black shirt, loose-fitting outfit . . . tight-fitting, etc. Suddenly I saw myself, in the mirror, looking at myself, with all this world around me, but really only me in there, in the mirror, and all I could think of was "If I was overeating, I wouldn't be doing this." Well, that's true. If I was overeating I would be considering where to shop . . . which store had seen the least of me this week. Where the next Ben & Jerry's truckload sale was going to be. It's just what it sounds like; a big fat truck full of fatty ice creams would pull up along a curb somewhere and some thin pretty girls would stand around selling tubs of ice cream really cheap. The truck has pictures of cows all over it to signify the milk in the ice cream, but I think it mirrors the buyers. We were, most of us, large chubby women, with children of course, standing in a good-natured line, waiting like patient bovines to select our ten for nine dollars' worth. We probably all had spoons in our purses. That was one thing I gave up when I started my diet program—the spoon in the purse, clanking with the change in the bottom of the feed bag, ready for any kind of passing lard.

It's true since I have lost 22¼ pounds I have become a member of the human race again. People say hello to me again. Men in particular I notice are speaking to me.

"You got that all right?" they say when I am seen leaving the store with a bag in my arms. Or, "Here, lemme get that," when I am entering the post office and they are holding the door. One guy even waved to me on the street today as I drove past. I didn't even know him! It's true he might have mistaken me for somebody else, but the point is I am visible again. It's a charge to my adrenaline. But it's kind of terrifying too. Why am I visible 22¼ pounds smaller than before? What makes fat see-through? Who *are* Ben and Jerry?

Fake Ice Cream

8 to 10 large frozen strawberries
4 to 6 ice cubes beaten with a hammer in a plastic bag till the blender can grind them
3 or 4 packs of Equal sweetener

A few teaspoons of lemon juice
A few teaspoons of extract—vanilla, chocolate, strawberry

Grind all the above ingredients in blender (this will take some time if your blender is anything like *my* blender: grind; stop; mix with spoon; grind; etc.). Blend until smooth and ice creamlike. Pour into gorgeous eating vessel and garnish with a slice of strawberry and a sprinkle of Equal. Eat till your head aches. It's only 50 calories or something incredibly low like that. And it takes an hour to make, so you aren't eating during that time, which is doubly good.

My son, J.D., has a friend over today. (That's how we say someone is visiting: having someone "over".) The little boy is a lot like J.D. only he has a speech impediment, so J.D. is always saying "What did you say?" to him. So far, they have driven Shelley and her teenage friends out of the house, chased Grace all over the yard with plastic swords, taken kitchen knives and cut up the plastic swords and now are out trying to feed the cows pricker bushes through the fence. I guess boys are different from girls. Shelley flounced out of the house, brushing her hair and yelling "He's such a *pain*!" to me.

Leadbelly, Vermont, is a rich town. There is a section out here for the up-and-coming low income, but for the most part Leadbelly is for the rich.

For the past few days a woman whom I justly owe for a service she rendered has been calling me asking for the money. I should pay her. I must pay her. And yet, I *can't* pay her. I tried to explain to her what poverty means.

"It's like if I told you to have an orgasm while you were walking down the street," I said. "Let's say everybody in town was having orgasms while they were strolling about and you couldn't. I mean, could you? No. Well, it's like that. You would feel great shame that you couldn't have an orgasm when everybody else was able to do it and I was all upset that you weren't, so of course you would feel terrible but what could you do? Nothing." I paused. *"That's* what it's like to be broke." I said.

That's not really what it's like to be broke and I didn't really say that to anyone. But it's a thought.

Lunch ################################

3 diet crackers spread with 2 ounces white chicken
1/2 teaspoon diet dressing
1 tall, frosty glass water
Tea with 1 pack Equal sweetener

Place chicken, dressing and crackers on elegant bone china. Serve icy water in etched glass goblet. Arrange flowers on table with teapot and read *Family Circle* while you eat, staring at full-color photos of Chicken L'Orange and Meaty Lasagna until you feel yourself climbing into the magazine. Follow up with relaxation techniques.

Which is more important, men or food? I have often asked myself this and still no answer rings in my head, just "Whatever's in front of you! Whatever's available!"

The children are gearing up for their annual Halloween party, which, it turns out, is tomorrow night. How time, like a witch, flies. J.D. wanted to be Odin, the all-father, for Halloween but I haven't made his suit yet so he is stuck being a cowboy for the party. Last year I made him a Lone Ranger suit that was truly a work of mother-art. But it took me hours to convince him the Lone Ranger was a notable character. He'd never heard of him.

"I'm the long raider," he went around saying, his sister Grace trailing behind in a Tonto suit. Anyway, this year the party crept up on me. I'm guilty of not cleaning the house in preparation. I'm guilty of spending the crepe paper money on diet Cokes for myself.

Good Mother Recipe ⌗⌗⌗⌗⌗⌗⌗⌗⌗⌗⌗⌗⌗⌗⌗⌗⌗⌗⌗⌗⌗⌗⌗

1. *1 or more children, the more the more saintly*
2. *Many holiday parties, inviting all the neighborhood*
3. *Classroom cupcakes, cookies, etc., at the drop of a hat*
4. *When accused of not doing enough, do more*
5. *Read 10 or more books aloud per night to all the children*

Add children to mother quickly, not stopping to blend. Stir in the rest of the above at an alarming rate. Heat to the boiling point, making sure the mother does not collapse as this will make the finished product tough.

I've been crying again this morning. Not because the cat pooped behind the stove, though that sometimes makes me cry, but because I read in the paper this tragic account of a woman waiting ten years to see her rapist convicted. I couldn't help it. Even now, the thought of her fists in the air and her happy face when they called out "Guilty" makes me cry. Something ruined in the air, something not right and never will be. It made me feel guilty for joking about rapists. It made me feel awful that I said anything cheery on the subject. How could I? Nothing is funny; absolutely nothing anymore. It is all black and gray and worn out and polluted. Everything hurts someone's feelings. There are too damn many people in the world. There is too much to feel guilty about. My heart breaks over everything. I'm here in this sorry hovel by an old dump in Nowhere, U.S.A., weeping over something that didn't happen in Leadbelly; didn't even happen recently. It's just that it happened. That these sad things happen. And who is the chief who cares? We need a person like a town crier who would run around weeping and reciting the sorrow as it comes about. Someone who would be in charge of caring. Like the old whipping boy of yore, he would (or she would) be responsible for sobbing over shattered glass, murdered lovers, dogs that had to be put to sleep, children who were unloved, stolen merchandise.

There is no time anymore. Everything is wrapped up in red tape and endless lines. To go to the grocery store for a can of dog food means waiting twenty minutes or more in line, waiting fifteen minutes or more in traffic. It all sucks up your minutes like milk from a straw . . . suddenly the day is over and you have accomplished zip. Well, unless you count the three trips to the children's school, the trip to the vet, the trip to the post office, and that can of dog food you had to go all the way back to town for. When you are home you are wandering around with your junk mail, unsure of where to put it . . . what will you do with the MCI long-distance cardholder card they sent you free? What will you do with the application for the job you had been interested in but now you aren't sure about? Where will all these important bills that you can't pay right now go? And the children's applications for art class; book club; letters from teachers that must be signed . . . a few magazines you love to look at, filled with steaming piping oozing foods that you aren't allowed to eat . . . where can all this stuff go?

The phone rings while you walk around holding large parcels of papers.

"Hello?"

"Hello. May I speak to Gabby?" Sounds friendly. First name basis.

"This is Gabby."

"Gabby Fulbriten, this is Fibs Plumbing. *When are you going to pay?*"

I can't stop crying suddenly. Was it the raped woman who so sadly had won little and was thanking God? Or was it the $3.50 it cost to buy J.D. a box of cereal? No matter how much I make checking out or modeling for painters, I never have anything. I remain in abject poverty. The Volvos in town pass me on route 6 filled with clean, bored kids, the mothers all slightly blond, thin, aerobic-bodied, aging beauties . . . graduates from the local elite college . . . handsome husbands busy being successful. I wonder how much these Volvos cost? And how do they all know what the *in* car will be each year? This year the brown

Volvo outlasts any other car in town. Everybody who's anybody has one. I'm not anybody but I cry as they parade past like a line to a funeral, lights on in the afternoon, children in seatbelts, life together, home clean. They pass me and they mutter but I don't hear them because my kids are all fighting over who has to sit in the back with the dog that's dying.

Oh salt tears. Oh tears of humankind. Oh tears for love and tears for parents and tears for death. Oh brokenhearted and shame tears. Oh tears of longing and tears of anguish. Helpless tears. Frightened tears. What tears are falling where? Who will be town crier?

I guess I ought to admit Shelley and I have a stormy relationship. Today we had another rotten day, Sunday, with me asking her to practice her saxophone and Shelley talking for hours on the phone to her friends, saying, "Like, did you see me when I said that? Like . . . gol, I mean . . ." and me in the background saying *"Get off the phone!* Shelley?" I suppose with the younger children it's easier to win. When J.D. wanted me to sew him a Ninja Turtle suit for Halloween all I said was "I can't. We don't have enough money for the shell part."

When Shelley and I fight I imagine hitting her sometimes. I think, "How easy it would be to slug her. Then I would get arrested and they would put Shelley in a foster home where she would probably get mistreated. *Then* she'd be sorry!" When Shelley is mad at me, of course she can't do much about it (neither can I though) except tell me to shut up and that she hates her life. But then she goes up to her room, slams the door and writes another story for English class in which the main character, a teenage girl, gets killed. Or the mother dies. She has oodles of these stories, which she won't let me see but which she tells me about.

"The mother died two pages ago," Shelley will say, coming into the kitchen where I am baking illegal oatmeal cookies.

"I'm on page ninety-five of this story and the mother made it all the way to page ninety-three. Can you believe it? Usually the mother dies in the beginning."

I say wow, I can't believe she's written so much, and I go back to licking the bowl.

Today, Shelley and I fought over practicing and over her friends calling too much and over the fact that I never do anything she wants me to do.

"Name one thing I got to do today," she says triumphantly. *"Just one."*

"It's Sunday," I remind her. "We never do anything on Sunday. It's the day we all stay home and be together."

"Yeah, right," she says, and stomps to her room. A

few minutes later she comes out when I am putting the finishing touches on some high-calorie dessert and says, "What's that disease teenagers get that kills them? You know . . . cystic something?"

"Cystic fibrosis," I say, shaking my head. The icing is getting hard and J.D. is complaining.

"I wanted purple icing," he says, stepping on the old dog. The dog moves silently away, a black and silver ghost of her former self, and suddenly I am filled with guilt. What if Shelley got some awful disease? What a heel I am. What kind of mother am I? Besides fat, I mean.

"When you get that, how long before you die?" Shelley calls down the stairs.

"About three pages," I respond gloomily. Maybe it's the fact that it's going to snow that has all of us in an uproar. Actually, lately I've been feeling like the planet is slowing down . . . sometimes I can feel the spinning of the Earth and it frightens me. What if the scientists know more than they are telling us and we are all about to come to a screeching halt and be thrown into outer space, hurtling like rockets, exploding, without being able to at least hold the children's hands as we all die . . . ? Some nights I am so sure of this that I can't sleep. I lie in dread . . . this is so much worse than lying in bed and imagining a killer man coming in through the window. This fear outweighs anything like those old fears. This is fear of extinction.

Instant uncontrollable obliteration. And I suppose part of it comes from knowledge of our ailing planet and part of it comes from rage.

Rage is a funny thing. It seeps into you when you think you can control it. Like saying something mean when you aren't feeling mean can suddenly make you very angry. Rage is like Jell-O; it takes the shape of whatever it is in and solidifies enough to be seen. There's a just dessert.

Wieners 'n' Rage ¤¤¤¤¤¤¤¤¤¤¤¤¤¤¤¤¤¤¤¤¤¤¤¤

1. *Fear of extinction, coming from the fact that you are the mother of a teenager and so rightly imagine yourself disappearing*
2. *Mini hot dogs steeped in hot sauce and boiled till they split*
3. *Fear of having done everything wrong; that instead of making a pineapple quilt you should be cleaning; that instead of cleaning you should be talking to the teenager; that instead of talking you should be helping the kids with their homework*
4. *Small onion, diced*
5. *26 1/2 pounds lost and still you are fat; small amount of fury stirred with wooden spoon*

Slop everything together in a big chipped bowl and store in refrigerator till it hardens or gets spilled.

Remove and turn out on big platter, moistening with guilt for easy cleanup. Offer to all. Continue standing and serving until everyone has gone.

Crippled with indecision? Can't make a move without your mother's advice? Call Leadbelly, 555-Cringe.

I'm going to quit screwing around here and get to a meaty recipe.

Skewered Turkey Giblet Indecisiveness ######

1. *Small turkey, cut into giblet-size morsels*
2. *Small requests, a few decisions*
3. *Anxious voice of the mother in you, enough to form a paste*
4. *Mixed feelings*

Put turkey in roaster with onion. Cook up and eat while adding the rest of the ingredients in a double boiler. Mixed feelings should dominate the flavor; the mother's voice a subtle addition. The kettle should be black. While eating, consider the thirty-two pounds lost, the lack of luster in your life, the hungry eyes of your children, the neediness and uncomfortable feeling emoting from everything. Watch world go by. Remember, Thanksgiving is just around the corner!

Thanksgiving is just around the corner. I'm working today at a grocery at the other end of the state. They need some work done on their books and they're short on register workers. They got my name from the Hurry Up food mart, so I guess word is getting around that I can work a cash register and do books with accuracy and speed. The children, meanwhile, have been planning another party. It's their birthday and they have invited fourteen children to attend. I don't even have four chairs to put around the table . . . but somehow we will manage. Maybe I'll make it a Pilgrim-birthday Thanksgiving where everybody eats in a circle on the floor. Or maybe they can take their cake and wander around holding their plates. Or maybe I'll fall sick and cancel.

Thanksgiving is just around the corner. This means Christmas is just around the corner. This signals the old red flag of despair. How will I manage? Who will pay for the presents? Is Santa real? Who will give me something? Why doesn't any man love me?

Iggy Stains showed up. Did I mention that? Flew out from the West Coast with his carry-on luggage and arrived at my door, clean and pressed and scrubbed and thin from too much fasting. The Mormons fast a great deal. They fast one day a month to cleanse their bodies and to show God respect and they also fast whenever they want to know something they can't find the answer to in a book so they ask God. The only way to hear God is for their body to be empty, I think so the Holy Spirit can come and visit them. The

Spirit can't visit a chubby body easily, so they have to peel off some weight and empty out the ol' house for the Spirit to get in. Now that I have lost thirty-two pounds I think the Spirit should have plenty of room in me. I would like to ask God if I will ever find a man or will Saddam Hussein actually go to war and finish off all the little band of men we have left? I would like to ask God if there are perhaps men in other countries who are more available and willing than in America. I would like to know, say, if the Italian men are more willing to enter into a relationship with a single mother of three, or perhaps the English men on the isle of Great Britain? How about a Chinese man? A Nepalese? One from the Panama Canal? A Greek? How about a Galápago? Are there any men on Galápagos or is it all penguins?

> TIME IS RUNNING OUT! SDWM ON THE PATH OF SALVATION AND TRUTH LOOKS FOR SW SLIM, ATTRACTIVE, PRETTY, BLONDE OR BRUNETTE (SORRY, NO REDHEADS!), CHARMING, FUNNY (BUT NOT TOO FUNNY), WITTY, AMIABLE. MUST HAVE A DESIRE TO CAMP, HIKE, SKI, SWIM, FISH, SAIL AND ENJOY TRAVEL. NO CHILDREN, NO PETS, PROFESSIONAL WORKING WOMAN ONLY. PHOTO PLEASE! COME ON, I KNOW YOU'RE READING THIS!

Like fun she is. Any woman like *that* would be reading *The Wall Street Journal* over croissants and herbal tea with her aerobics suit on in a penthouse in New York City with her gorgeous husband flying in on a DC-10 at 4 P.M., you stupid SOB.

Dreams. Hester came down yesterday during the day while I was scrubbing the floors and told me her dream. Then she told me her daughter's dream. And while she told me, I remembered the dream I had had that night about a wonderful yard sale at my other neighbor's house where there were wax dolls and antique hats for sale. Everything was very cheap. There were angels carved around mirrors and I was buying everything. All this wonderful stuff right next to my house! Maybe what that means is the same thing Dorothy said in *The Wizard of Oz,* that if you go looking for something you're liable to find it right in your own backyard . . . that it's all right here anyway. Because I have been wanting to go looking. I have considered maybe leaving this area to find a man somewhere else, because it seems there are no men in my backyard. And a hopeless, awful depression has descended on me and I can't think what to do except leave.

In my backyard, the clothes swing crazily on the wash line: a Victorian nightgown, a boy's hunting jacket, some shorts left over from summer. They have been swinging there for almost a month. I can't get the enthusiasm to go out and whistle while I bring in dry clothes. I will probably let them freeze there in the coming cold nights and turn to cardboard figures, left hanging through the winter by clothespins on a rope.

The condominiums are almost finished. They are visible from my bedroom window, sticking up along the bluff like fingers of a giant. They are taller than the pine trees at the edge of the cow field. Someone came and sawed down the dead trees where the pileated woodpeckers used to roost. There are no birds around anymore. Not even a chickadee in my popple tree.

Christmas is coming now. Thanksgiving is finished, the turkey carcass thrown out with the disposable aluminum pan (I handed it ceremoniously to the garbage collector man. He looked at it awkwardly—no green bag to disguise the bald truth: we ate it, we pitch it, pan and all). I wander through the stores that are rapidly running out of everything, and I look at the gifts for sale. I listen to Christmas music played by a harp. I try to feel *something.* Anything. But there's only a dull buzz in my ears, a vague blah feeling. I look in my backyard again.

There is a shed that the kids wanted me to make into a playhouse. There is the sandbox under a pine tree that the kids wouldn't play in because spiders let themselves down by threads from the pine tree into the sandbox and frightened them. There is the garden space, bulldozed this past summer by my free bulldozer prize. Nothing grew there. There is an old trampoline turned upside down. There is the brown grass.

The first of December and still it hasn't snowed. Whether or not this is the effect of global warming doesn't seem to interest me. Perhaps poverty is making me blue. Or maybe the diet. I have lost thirty-three boring pounds, ho hum, and yet in the mirror a fat old woman still looks at me. I can't shake her or get rid of her. I suppose if I starve her long enough she will die, but maybe I will never love my reflection. Along with this quiet droning depression is an anxiety I cannot rid myself of either. The world will stop spinning. I will die if I try to leave Leadbelly, Vermont. The children will die if we change our everyday routine. Everything will die . . . a gruesome, terrifying death. And, of course, I still hear my old cancerous dog crying at the door, wanting to come in. Wanting out of her grave. Someone told me to let her go. But how can I? Me, who hired the killer to come in and do the job, who had my brother-in-law bury her in the backyard without my ever looking at the grave. How can I ever let her go? She will stand shivering on the porch near a bowl of frozen dog water, whining to come in, forever and ever. I will see her unsteady walk to the mailbox, the thin legs wobbling outside my bedroom window, her wheezing in the pantry. The murderer goes unpunished, caught or not. Why leave Leadbelly when everything you ever wanted is in your own backyard?

A policeman just knocked on my door. I could tell by the way he was standing that nobody had died. It was financial.

"Have you ever been issued a small claims court order?" he asked pleasantly, as my puli snarled behind me. My old dog wouldn't have snarled at a policeman. My old dog had a lot of respect for cops. Anyway, I thought Fibs Plumbing had thrown me to the lions, but it turned out to be some convenience store I had written a bad check to last year. The check was for nine dollars. I recall it as if it were yesterday, though of course it couldn't be yesterday because the bank closed my account months ago for bouncing checks. Anyway, I had tried to pay these people back but they wouldn't take the nine dollars. They wanted a twenty-five-dollar extra fee. That's all the rage now. They call them "bank fees," though the bank assured me it doesn't charge stores for customers' bounced checks. Anyway, there was this policeman being very nice to me. He said I could fill out this card and send it to the court explaining my situation. Then he looked around at the old crashing-in porch and left. I wondered if he was related to my neighbor Hester. Hester seems to be related to everybody around here. Then I thought, maybe everyone in town is laughing at me and tallying up how much I owe everyone. It's depressing how much one owes, no matter how many bills one pays. I mean, I pay the garbage people oodles of money and the electric company and the phone bill and the mortgage and the grocery and still these horrendous bills keep popping up and people are glaring at me from every store. The convenience store didn't stop at the nine dollars or the twenty-five-dollar bank fee. It added on twenty-five dollars for court costs and twenty dollars more for hiring the policeman. I didn't realize policemen got paid so much. Twenty dollars for two minutes? Now I owe almost one hundred dollars. Probably if I don't send the card in on time I'll be charged another twenty-five dollars for card-refusal-to-send-in charges.

Elvis sings on the tape player. I can't imagine why Priscilla left him, except maybe that he took drugs. But still, I would have stayed. I would stay with almost anyone who could afford to pay these bank fees at this point.

"I hear the bells, saying Christmas is near . . ." sings Elvis. Maybe I should marry Iggy Stains. Let's admit it, I'm not getting any younger and though I've lost thirty-three pounds, no man has thrown himself into my backyard. After all, Iggy has his good points. I told him when he was here about the art show downtown.

"There's this art show and many of the paintings are of me," I explained. "I am a model on the side, Iggy. Did you know that? It's fun. I mean, I don't take off my clothes or anything. I just wear interesting clothes and sit very still while all these painters paint me. I wonder if you'd like to stop down and take a look at the show?"

Iggy had arrived broke and I had to make him all

these lavish meals so he would know what a good cook I am—in case I decided to, he would still want to marry me.

"I'm taking an art class in school," he said, carefully picking a thread off his neat sweater. Iggy is very clean. "I'm afraid I'll have to drop the course, though, even if it is a requirement . . . because there's going to be a nude model coming in next month. I don't know for sure . . . but I'll have to talk to my bishop about it. It'll probably cause all kinds of unclean thoughts. I want to graduate but I don't want any unclean thoughts. Heavenly Father wouldn't like that!"

I was startled into silence. How could anyone think the way Iggy thought? "I'm sure your bishop will give you the go-ahead," I said finally. But Iggy shook his head.

"I don't know about that . . . sittin' there . . . looking at a naked lady. He'll probably have me drop the course, or just stay home that day. I'll have to talk to my teacher 'bout it. You wouldn't want me lookin' at no naked lady, would you?" Iggy stared at me with his large lidless eyes. I shrank from him, a feeling of grubbiness sweeping over me.

Something worrisome is in the air. I know it because it is being reflected in the children, and my neighbor. It might be that Operation Desert Shield, the Saddam

Hussein thing. Last night I dreamed aliens were coming and they called me for directions on how to get here. I was surprised at myself in the dream for telling them. Then I waited with the children for them to arrive. I knew it would be the end, but I was sure that even without my directions they would have found the planet.

Once you face death, *know* it, then I guess it will always be there. I mean, once the door has opened to death in your life, it will bound to be a recurring thing. My old dog was that door. When the euthanasia van arrived (actually, it turned out to be a Jeep) I was weeping but resolved. I had called them earlier that morning and given the man directions on how to get to my house. And so you see? The aliens had invaded.

Later, I called the woman who had first diagnosed the jugular cancer in my old dog five months ago. She was very sympathetic. I didn't cry on the phone to her. In fact, after all that crying, I felt rather jubilant. Guilt was mingled with my wild, unseemly happiness. I had held my dog when he gave her a sleeping potion, and she had, for the first time in years, seemed like her old self again . . . a puppy asleep in my arms. She snored and was not wheezing anymore. I had cried then for hours, and slowly this calm feeling came over me. I had faced death, inevitable death, and it was right.

"The vet was nice," I said, growing ever more joyful. "Is he married? I know that sounds awful, doesn't it? But he was so cute . . ."

The woman on the other end of the phone said, "Forget it. He's gay." This was disappointing, but I hung up still feeling good.

Only last night, I could hear my old dog shuffling around the kitchen. I could hear her peeing on the rug, could hear her coughing, whining. It filled me with horror . . . to think she will forever wander my house. Oh, treachery. Oh, trust and hope and treachery. Her eyes, glued nearly shut by illness, her barrel body weaving and staggering forever through my house, heavy with cancer, ravaged with cancer that was starving her. And then the aliens called and I said, "Well, you have to fly into New York, just west of the moon, and route eighty-nine will take you quite close to Leadbelly, Vermont. We're the place by the old dump. You can't miss it."

While I spoke, my children stared up at me with trusting eyes. Did they know I was killing them by this one phone call?

Where are all the men? I'll tell you where they are. They are all working for MCI Telecommunications Network. They hire them, I think, because a male voice is a rare sound these days, so when I pick up my phone and hear, "Uhh . . . may I speak to Gabby

Fulbriten?" in a deep, authoritative, but pleasant-sounding voice, I immediately say, "Yes, this is Gabby," and forgetting that no man would call me to ask me out or to say how much he likes me because I don't *know* any men. This can only be . . .

"Yes, Gabby, this is John, from MCI Telecommunications, and we are wondering, how are you enjoying your service?"

"You just called and asked me that two days ago," I say sullenly.

"Did we? Then . . . uhhh, I guess this phone call is irrelevant," he says, his voice like the voice of an old boyfriend of mine. I long to communicate.

"No, no," I say. "I did want to ask you about your evening rates that apply only to the weekends . . ." and we are off and running, John explaining in his man's voice about thirteen cents a minute and me giggling like a teen over the eleven cents a minute after nine but before five weekends and weekdays throughout. All too soon, it is over, but he has promised to mail me a chart to hang by my phone that reiterates all that he has just said. Sort of a Hallmark card that says just how you feel toward someone else, written by a total stranger and purchased by *you.*

"Thank you, John. Thank you, John," I say, and John, before hanging up, says, "No problem."

Possible Places the Men Might Be Hiding:

1. Saudi Arabia, Desert Shield

2. At MCI Telecommunications warehouses throughout the country

❦

My sister Nina called me the other day from her farm in New Hampshire. We were very close as children, but to be honest, since we became adults we almost have too much in common to get along anymore. It's like talking to myself when we converse. Although we are several years apart in age and have different hair color, people can't tell us apart in Leadbelly when she comes over to visit. Our voices are identical over the phone . . . Nina's kids look like my kids—it's that odd sister thing where townfolk can't tell who's who.

"Did you hear about the mercury thing?" she asks me over the phone.

"No, what?" I say.

"Oh, God, it's really awful. All our silver fillings are made of mercury . . . It's so deadly the dentists keep it in vials marked POISON and use gloves to handle it . . . then they fill our mouths with it." I am wrapping the last Ninja Turtle for J.D.'s stocking as we speak.

"Mercury, like in thermometers?" I ask. Nina says yes.

"And it causes total memory loss, and all kinds of weird, horrible things. And it's worse to remove it because of the fumes . . . but after you get all the fillings out it does get better."

"I don't have teeth," I say. "I eat with my fillings. There's no way they could remove mercury from my mouth. My face would collapse."

I stuff an orange in the toe of J.D.'s stocking and begin filling it with candy and chocolates and small presents. Christmas always makes me suicidal and anxious at once. Anxiety because whatever I bought is not enough and is not quite right, and suicidal because I hate the feeling of purchasing till you are broke and coming home to a dirty house filled with dirty, cranky children and no man. No man. No man.

> SANTAS WANTED FOR DEPARTMENT STORE IN GREATER LEADBELLY AREA. MALE, THE BIGGER THE BETTER. WE PROVIDE SUIT. MUST BE DEPENDABLE.

No man. No dependable big man at all. Just candy canes and a tree that is already dry and losing its needles. Just hundreds of presents stuffed under my bed so the kids won't see. Just eggnog in the refrigerator and rain coming in the porch because it doesn't snow in Vermont anymore due to the greenhouse effect. "I am so vexed that every part about me quivers. Scurvy knave!" (Nurse in *Romeo and Juliet*).

I can't even remember what it feels like to be in love. I am almost repelled by the thought anymore . . . isn't that *awful*? What could be more humiliating than to discover passion and love repulse you? Or at least petrify you? Perhaps, in my thirties I am growing frigid.

"Frigid" used to be a common thing for people to say about women they didn't like. "He finally had to leave her after thirty-two years of marriage . . . she was frigid, you know," and that sort of thing. Then "frigid" became "radical feminist." "He had to leave her after thirty-two years of marriage . . . well, she turned into a radical feminist and just turned his life upside down." Let's see, that would have been in the seventies. In the eighties, the taboo woman was an ambitious, self-motivated bitch. "He had to finally save himself after thirty-two years of marriage because she went back to school and got her degree and became an ambitious, self-motivated bitch who was willing to crawl over anybody to get to the top and just put her family on the back burner."

What will the nineties bring? Now that the men have left us because we were so awful, what will they say about women of the nineties? I have a glimpse of what: "I don't even speak to women anymore," they might say. "They're all divorced with kids and harboring all this resentment toward the fathers and you can see the desperation in their eyes . . . brrr! It gives me the creeps!"

"I was thinking of having all my teeth pulled," Nina says. "At least I would get my memory back . . ."

"Yeah, but then what? Maybe this is part of the plan in a big way . . . maybe we need to lose our memories in order to be better robots in the work world and in order to stomach smarmy television shows. Anyone who can remember the way it used to be would never want to live the way it is now." I have put together Grace's new dolly cradle and in it, under the tree, I place her new rubber baby. She had wanted a glass one, but I didn't think it would last long around here.

"I feel like my mouth has betrayed me," Nina was saying. "I can't sleep, I have such anxiety over it."

"You have that, too?" I ask. It's almost midnight and I am finally finished with wrapping. The tree, though growing bald, is pretty, with the colored lights and delicate ornaments. But really, nothing is exciting to me tonight. This languishing depression that descended around the holidays has not left me. Is it worry over the planet? Or is it just a dying out of more feelings?

"This sounds crazy," I say to Nina, "but I've been terrified the planet is slowing down. I've been off balance for months. I start to keel over, especially when I go into the kitchen near the cookstove. It feels like the room is caving in."

Nina sighs into the phone. "It might be your teeth," she says.

Before Grace and J.D. were born, I lived with their father in a cabin in Vermont—Jefferson Dutton Pantaloni and myself, living in this dilapidated place with no money, and he decides that in order to save our faltering relationship, we have to have a child. Shelley, of course, is living with us and she chimes in saying yes yes she wants a baby sister. "It could be a brother," I warn her, trying to argue them out of it. "It could?" she says, "Well, that's all right." Shelley and Jefferson didn't get along as well as they could have. Shelley didn't like the fact that he was always around . . . wouldn't let us have a minute alone like mothers and daughters do . . . he was jealous. While we lived there he called his mother every other night to check in. They were a very tight-knit Italian family, only the mother wasn't Italian and the parents were divorced, but otherwise they were the typical Italian family in New York . . . father in politics, mother an aging beauty, grandparents in Brookline speaking mostly Italian, and two sisters who were oblivious. Jefferson himself was sort of oblivious but brilliant. He played wild compositions on the piano and wrote bad poetry and chipped in financially, working as a bartender in Leadbelly. Yes, we even then lived near Leadbelly.

The trouble was, I knew nothing would keep us together. His parents didn't approve of me at all and we fought all the time over money and space. They say couples fight more over money but I wonder if it's a spatial thing. People don't have the *room* they once did—like in the Victorian era, everybody had his or her own wing on the house. Now you're lucky to get a tiny Sheetrocked room with one shrimpy window. It's like the condos they're building—the floor plan is the size of a Victorian bedroom. Of course, back through history, there were castles to live in with one's own turret and plenty of outdoors to gallop around in. Nowadays, moose are on the highway and people are cramped together, fighting.

Because the cabin was so tiny, there was only enough room for one desk and he wanted it, but he already had the living-room area for his baby grand piano. And I wanted the desk because I was taking a through-the-mail course on bookkeeping (which later developed into my job at Hurry Up). Even now, just mentioning that time evokes such feelings! Fury, for one. He insisted that I get pregnant . . . I didn't want to . . . and when I got pregnant, I was very angry about it. One day he held me down on the floor and screamed in my face, *"You must have this child!"* I felt like Rosemary's Baby.

So week after week went by, he kept a close eye on me to make sure I didn't sneak off and get an abortion . . . when I was four months along, he announced he was leaving. "I have a doctor's appointment today," I said, glaring at him from a corner of the cabin. We had just fought again about the desk and both our papers were all over the floor. "Doctor?" he said, airily.

"A checkup . . ."

"It's too late for that," he said.

"Not an abortion . . . a checkup, to hear the baby's heartbeat."

I can't remember where Shelley was but she wasn't there right then. She must have been in the yard. Anyway, Jefferson picked up his briefcase that he was always carrying around and said he was going to go pack. I threw myself on him and screamed, but he was very calm about the whole thing. He said it just wouldn't work out. And he refused to stay another night. But, he said, he would call later in the week to see how the checkup went. An hour later, with his bags packed, he stood at the door of our shack. He was really into vitamins because he didn't eat meat and he had just taken his niacin. Niacin made him turn bright red. "Well, I'm off," he said, grabbing the doorknob. I had put Dolly Parton on and her song "I Will Always Love You" was playing.

"Don't leave me!" I begged, but really I didn't mind so much. He was so very thin from eating only bulgur and rice and his face and hands were beet red from the niacin and he had hold of his briefcase, which I knew contained only health food and bad poetry . . . I guess I sound mean. That must be why he left me. Anyway, he *did* leave. His father by some miracle showed up (Jefferson must have called him). And his father and my mother (who also was there by the way) had a fight in the road in front . . . not a physical fight . . . my mother yelled, "You shouldn't let your son be so irresponsible!" and his father laughed and said, *"Ma che cosa?"* and my mother screamed

"You should have been nicer to my daughter . . . you should have helped them . . ."

And his father said, *"Ci sono tende dappertutto!"* which means "There are tents everywhere" and that's not what he said, but he said *something* in Italian, which nobody understood. The only thing I can say is *Ci sono tende dappertutto* . . . There are tents everywhere.

Jefferson came back a month or two later to help out until the twins were born. He tried to be nice. But I knew his parents were disgusted with the whole thing. His parents were against it and you know one can't fight one's parents . . . like my mother. She just didn't want her daughters to get married after what happened to her. "They're all dangerous," she told me. She meant men.

Shelley sat with me in the hospital after they were born. She was six and in first grade. We couldn't hold them because they were rather sickly, but we sat together and discussed it all. "Will we have enough room in the car for them?" she asked.

"The hospital is loaning us some infant seats," I said.

"Why do they have to be under the incubator?"

"They're still too small . . ." I said. We were drinking ginger ale from little paper cups. The hospital room was warm and stuffy. Shelley was staying with my mother at the Ronald McDonald house nearby . . .

"Where's Jefferson?" she wanted to know.

"I don't know," I said.

Christmas came and went. I went to a few local parties, nothing major. One was at the single female veterinarian's house. She was the vet who had first told me about the euthanasia van that eventually put my old rotting dog to sleep. On the night of her party, the biggest snowstorm of the decade dumped mountains of slippery snow all over the roads. When I called her to cancel because of the dangerous conditions, she sounded a little drunk.

"Don't tell me you're calling to cancel," she said, breathless, into the phone. "Two thirds of the people I invited have canceled."

"No, I'm not canceling," I lied. "I was just calling to say I'm on my way and to look for me in a snow bank if I'm not there in ten minutes. Also, is it okay if I bring J.D. and Grace? Shelley is visiting friends in Boston and I don't have the nerve to leave them alone out here by the old dump."

"Well," the female vet said, "no other kids are coming . . . but . . . sure."

"Thanks," I said.

"I'm not going to baby-sit, though," she added.

"Oh, no. I wouldn't want that," I said. "Could they watch a movie or something? Do you have a VCR?"

Silly question. Everyone in the world of Leadbelly has a VCR. I bet everyone in Vermont has a VCR. Even people who can't afford anything other than twenty-five-cent boxes of macaroni and cheese have VCRs. They are the poor *and* the rich's necessities, though the poor watch their movie on the VCR with a nineteen-inch screen and the rich have a room set up in the house like a theater with a thirty-two-inch wall screen and a popcorn machine. (This is all conjecture.)

Poor Versus Rich—Who Really Has It All?

1. Rich. Rich people have homes and cars that never need a tow truck. Rich people have lots of things in the pantry, like olives in jars and Scotch whisky if other rich people drop by. Rich people have jobs that make them richer and that don't wear them down to a bare, humble wire. Rich people have bright children because they send them to loads of enriching classes after school and most of the kids get to go to private schools where learning is fun and your feelings are considered important. Rich people have clean clothes that fit and appropriate clothes for the occasion.

2. Poor. The poor tend to be angry. They often shout at their children over nothing because they are ashamed of their lot in life. The poor have humble dwellings like small bungalow houses or narrow tin trailers. Prefab houses are popular among the poor

and many now live in shoddy-made condominiums. The poor people have cars that they nurse along, but often a smoking Pinto or a kaput Escort will be parked alongside the road with a poor person hovering nearby like an embarrassed bee near burdock. Poor people have several boxes of twenty-five-cent macaroni and cheese in the cupboard and some old yogurt in the refrigerator. Often, poor people will have more food in stock on hand than the rich people. That is because the poor comfort themselves with food. Advertisements on television tell the poor that if they buy green-wrapped chocolate candies they will be leaning back in leather-bound chairs in front of a cozy fire with a towering, beautiful man in the background holding a present. None of this is true. The candy will just make the poor person fatter and pimply and the money wasted on these unnutritious items will mean the twenty-five-cent macaroni box dinner will have to be made without milk. Have you ever had Grand Union macaroni and cheese made with just water? Poor people usually don't work, but if they do work their jobs are meaningless and boring. Rote and predictable and humiliating. This is natural and the way the world goes round. Rich people would not want to work in factories soldering wires together or be the sweeper in the dime store or stand on the back of the garbage truck, shouting "Back it up! Keep going!" all day. But the poor, we accept our lot. We have traditionally accepted it throughout time. You see poor children in cheap clothes (or expensive clothes if the poor person is trying to hide the poverty, which is the new thing these days), and you see they have yellow teeth and unbrushed hair. The shoes are a telltale sign of lack of money. Kids might wear CB jackets and fancy hats and brand-new boots, but when you check out their shoes you'll see the poverty. Poor children are often not invited into challenging school programs because they are not rich and cannot afford to be sent to after-school art classes, after-school gymnastic classes, after-school piano lessons, and after-school viola. Generally, after school they go to a huge, boring day-care program where you can peer in the windows and see them all lined up at long plastic-coated tables in a big yellow room drinking watered-down apple juice from paper cups and looking dully at each other.

As a member of the poor myself, I question these weird rules but I see most of it is unchangeable. And though the rich people have quite different lots from mine, they are not necessarily *nice* lots. I personally would have a very hard time being rich. I would never be able to enjoy my money, knowing that such sorrow and longing existed all around me. I could not relax in my large, leather-bound swivel chair with a box of green-wrapped chocolates knowing that a family like I used to be was down the street eating powdery macaroni and cheese made without the right ingredients. I would be filled, I'm sure, with a continual sense of horror. So I rest my case that it is better to be poor and without guilt than rich and without shame.

"Get in the car, J.D. *Get in the car!* Why don't you hear me?" J.D. was wiping snow off the headlights of the car in the black swirling night. The snow had covered everything in the yard and made our place by the dump seem frosty clean and almost country elegant. The woodpile looked stacked under all the snow. The house was cheery with the kitchen light left on. Grace and J.D. were making too much noise as we drove to the vet's party, so I used an old trick of my mother's.

"Oh my God oh my God we're going off the road!" I screamed, and I turned the wheel just a little toward the edge of the highway. "We're sliding!" I said.

"Oh my God!" whispered J.D. Then they both got very quiet and the rest of the short ride was just the sound of the windshield wipers trying to get the ice off the window . . . and me sighing heavily because I feel especially gloomy at Christmastime.

I had asked the vet on the phone if my dog was invited to the Christmas party and she had said, without humor, "No." When we got there, I parked in a huge snowdrift and, as they say in Nancy Drew books, "took a mental picture of where the road was," because it was fast disappearing. The vet greeted us at the door with a Scotch in her hand. Or maybe it was a straight vodka. I can't tell drinks by their color.

"Glad you could make it . . . hey, kids," she said, and took my children off to the next room. I followed.

"Gee, there seems to be quite a few here already," I said, looking out into her living room. Several thin women were sitting on one couch eating peanuts, or something, from a bowl. One large guy, and I mean *very* large guy, was strolling back and forth from the kitchen to the living room with bread sticks in his hand.

"Hey, kids, what do you wanna watch?" the vet asked. My kids were staring at her.

"Do you have cartoons?" J.D. asked.

"Anything," I said. "Just put on anything . . . You don't have to do this. I can help them," I said.

"Sure, I have cartoons," the vet went on, ignoring me. She was slurring some of her *t*s. "Wanna play with toys? Look at all the toys," she said. My kids looked around the quiet room.

"I'll do this," I repeated. Then the large guy came in and offered me a drink.

"Wanna drink? How's the snow out there?" he asked, drawing me out of the den and into the living room where the thin women were all together on the couch. "That there's Carrie, she's Mandy, and I don't know who the hell that one is," he joked, pointing to all three of the women.

An enormous woman appeared beside the big man. "Honey, I have to get back," she whispered.

"Well, go," he said. He was staring at me. I began to feel great despair. Christmastime does that to me. And fat men who think I would be interested in them.

Why do I hate fat men? Well, I don't. If they were fat and brilliant and charming I guess I would like them all right. It's just that fat people (fat men) tend to be gross and thick and stupid . . . like their fat is insulating their brains and disconnecting them from understanding. For instance, fat men think they are attractive, in dirty enormous jeans that hang down and expose their hairy fat bellies. They often wear T-shirts with slogans splashed across the front. NOBODY'S GONNA BURN THIS ONE!, with a flag printed on the back. Or GOD DIED AND LEFT ME BOSS, or just a cartoon of Fred Flintstone and YABA DABA DOO beneath it. Maybe smart people who are fat don't come out of their dwellings out of embarrassment, so the only fat men I ever see are fat idiots. I also hate fat because I myself battle it every day. I swell up like a tomato on the vine, plumping out daily, and then when I can hardly stumble around and my knees crack and my back aches and my breathing is labored, I go to Diet Center and they carve me back down to a size 10 again. But every day that I am not indulging, I am fighting. I am speaking in hushed and hurried tones to the refrigerator . . . "No, thank you. I am not hungry. I am not going to eat that ice cream. I don't even *like* string cheese. Close the door!" Funny thing about my refrigerator . . . it has a weak front now, and so if you walk past it, the door swings open to greet you. The same thing with my pantry shelves. They are all built on a slant, so when you go in the room everything falls off the shelves and demands that you pick it up, if not to eat it, at least to put it away again. So my food follows me, badgers me, and I am never rid of that feeling that if I just have a few beautifully wrapped goodies while I sit in a ladderback chair in front of the beautiful tung-oiled table, I will become those happy people in the *Country Journal* magazines who have warm, fulfilled lives surrounded by rich tones and fatty foods.

Consumer Cry Croissants ¤¤¤¤¤¤¤¤¤¤¤¤¤¤¤¤

1. *1 consumer who cares about the Earth*
2. *too little time to investigate anything, too little time to make your* own *bread, butter, cereal, whatever. No time even to complain to the companies, no time to do anything but shop, eat, and run off to work or to pick up the kids*
3. *Packaged goods wherever you turn*
4. *Locked-in-freshness seals, plastic resealable caps, plastic pull seals for easy top removal*
5. *Aluminum, FDC number anything, MSG, aerosol, etc.*

Place person who cares in 6-inch saucepan and add lack of time first. This will cause all other ingredients to fall into place better. And after all, since the aluminum and coloring and MSG aren't spoiling the immediate moment, why not? As person who cares becomes hardboiled, remove from heat and place in front of regular television sitcoms. *America's Funniest Home Videos* and *America's Funniest People* will give the recipe a gelatinous, somewhat soggy character. Roll out with rolling pin on floured surface and fold into neat triangles. Stab with toothpick to let steam escape. Several doses of radiation in the microwave and remove pins from body of product while still warm. Result? A marvelous, flaky croissant with virtually nothing in it of any substance . . . a hollow interior that can be filled with any chemical or synthetic materials.

A thin, pocked-faced woman came up to me as I was edging toward the TV room where Grace and J.D. were sitting. "You're Gabby Fulbriten, right?" she said. She was holding a glass with whiskey and no ice. I thought maybe she was a creditor.

"Well . . ." I began.

"You used to live with Jeff, didn't you?" she was smiling at me in an all-knowing way . . . I looked confused probably.

"Who?"

"Jeff. You lived with him, right? In an old cabin? Jeff Pantaloni." My body relaxed . . . I nodded yes.

"I didn't know who you meant when you said 'Jeff.'" He always insisted on being called . . ."

"Yeah, my sister married him. He is one funny character, lemme tell you!" The woman leaned toward me and laughed. The large guy was standing behind her, staring at me still. I felt nauseated suddenly as though I had mixed Champagne and gin.

"No kidding," I said. I moved into the TV room. The pocked woman tilted her head . . . "They live in China," she went on. I coughed.

"China," I repeated. How far away can one get? The large guy stepped closer. "I have to leave," I called out, to no one in particular. He stepped up.

"I'll give you a ride . . . got a truck out front," he said.

"Oh, these your kids?" the woman went on. J.D. looked up from the floor where he and Grace were sitting together. "Baily, God give me a ride if you're going . . . I've got to head out too . . . got room for all of us?"

"That's okay," I said, pushing past both of them, holding Grace and pulling J.D. behind me . . . "I've got a car."

"Maybe I'll see you later," the guy said. "That weren't my wife you saw . . ."

It was snowing harder when we left. The twins fell asleep on the way home and I had to carry them one at a time to bed.

What a busy January so far! With the war in Iraq and all, there seems to be no time left outside of worrying. *Newsweek* calls this decade the Decade of Anxiety. I read that while I was waiting for a dentist appointment. This is certainly the age of No Time. While waiting for a root canal, I overheard a woman saying, "I'm driving to the other side of the state to be checked for allergies. I'll be with Dr. Foley all day," and the dentist saying he had gone through a battery of tests, too, and discovered he was allergic to dust and had a low tolerance for ragweed. "I'll barely have time to get to my aerobics class," the woman said. Top the day off with a trip to the VCR store to browse through new releases and one could say one did nothing all day.

The people in Iraq, it seems, are also in the age of anxiety. We see them throughout early January on our television sets, gathering fruit to stockpile for the impending war. Bananas to ward off a nuclear bomb. Grapes and apples during those especially long air-raid strikes. There are two worries going on at once. One worry is that Saddam Hussein will miraculously beat us, like in *Henry the Fifth* the English beat the French when there were thousands more French than English and the English were hungry and ragged. Surprise! The United States of Arabia? Would we all be systematically killed or would the Arabs let the women live? You think about these things . . . Would the Arabs like one better if one was blond or brunet? Would they want a chubby woman or a thin one? Would children be slaughtered? Could I hide my family? Would the Arabs even check Vermont, let alone Leadbelly? I mean, it's such a small town! There would be much more to pillage in New York. Then the other worry is that we will blow up Iraq and murder all those little children whom *Newsweek* took pictures of . . . all those people amassing fruit. All those dusty, turbanned people who seem to have no inkling what the "civilized world" is capable of . . . of course, Saddam Hussein himself is a butcher, and he is followed by fanatics who are desperate for improvement. But what if we blow them off the planet and it changes the course of the planet circling the sun and we are thrown closer to Mercury? Then we will all be in the desert and there will be no shield to protect us. THE AGE OF ANXIETY, *Newsweek* said. It listed all the things people were worried about. Banks, loans, mortgages, garbage crisis, fuel, environment. They seemed to skip over the things I am concerned about. They had many pages on fuel and the Gulf and banking, but they just skimmed garbage and air. *Newsweek* is very depressing. Even their ads are depressing. There are ads for saving a child for a cup of coffee . . . but when even that obligation is too strainful? What then? It is like the Gulf crisis. Everything is like the Gulf crisis. There is no choice and there is a choice. We could bomb them. We could starve them out. We could wait. We could move quickly. But there are really no choices in this instant food, instant housing, instant families, instant war world.

A few days ago my Diet Center counselor invited me to sing with her at a grade school. She's a substitute music teacher. In this small class, in the front row, a little wizened girl was covering her ears during "The Rattling Bog" song. She kept shaking her head and saying, "Too loud, too loud. Too much noise." I finally took her back to her class, whispering to her as we walked down the halls. I patted her head and she smiled at me. She had Down's syndrome. But I could see how the music had really hurt her. She was suffering in the front row with her ears covered like a child might sit in a bomb shelter during an air raid. Or in an open market, covering their ears, holding fruit.

And so January flies by, with no time, the time of anxiety, and Shelley has a persistent cough, and J.D. stays home from school because of a sore throat, and Grace complains of aches and pains. I myself am nearly crippled with a backache today, but I think it is due to my lousy mattress. However, there is the possibility that Saddam has already sent germ warfare over to our country without anyone's noticing and it causes everyone not to drop dead but to feel crummy and not care. That would be a way to win a war; kill the enemy with apathy. Give them aches.

It almost seems, in this decade of anxiety, that nothing else exists anymore . . . that the condominiums for the low-income people have all but disappeared in the face of war; that the old town dump is never visited by guys roaring up to take a leak; that even the personals have vanished and the newspapers are filled only with where you can dedicate a song to a guy in the Gulf. "To send your request to your loved one in the Persian Gulf, write Operation Desert Shield, AFRTS" or "To call your loved one in the Desert Shield operation, dial these codes first . . ." It seems like everyone has left our country and is living on the sands of Saudi Arabia. Even Hester has relatives there. "Seems a shame they won't let our boys celebrate Christmas or Hannukah or Thanksgiving . . ." people complain. "It will be awkward there during their holy days of Ramadan." The world is not the world; it is something else. It is a building of tension and excitement and dread and horror. It is no longer condominiums or grocery store checkout stories . . . It is one massive machine working for the one final result. There is no room in this new world for individual remarks or histories. It is the long arm of the robot, reaching across continents, reaching, reaching, we are all attached like tug-of-war, stretching, we will win collectively or we will fall in the river. No one will just put down the rope.

Well, lose some, gain some. That's an old saying that refers to yo-yo dieting. After two batches of cookies and three servings of chili, I am ready to jump out of a window. Why is there not enough incentive in my life to lose weight?

Single fat woman seeks man. Must have better qualities than the man in *All's Well That Ends Well.*

There's a guy for you, Shakespeare's Count Rousillon. He is forced to marry this beautiful, intelligent, obedient daughter of a doctor, and he hates her because she isn't rich. So he dumps her with his mother and goes off to fight a war in Iraq, or somewhere, and she follows him there, disguised as a pilgrim. She discovers he is sleeping around and so she tricks him into sleeping with her and she gets pregnant. When he thinks she is dead, he goes back to his mother and she shows up again, pregnant with his child, and after being threatened with jail he apologizes and they settle down together.

All's well that ends well. Lose some, gain some. A bird in the hand is worth two in the bush. Shit happens.

If only I could overcome my faults! If I could stop overeating, stop yelling at the kids, stop sitting like a lump on a log and be productive somehow . . . but I can no more rid myself of my faults than I can get a man. Than Bush can flush Saddam out of his bunker. You know, it all rolls along and we have little to do with any of it.

The Mormons are having a gathering at the church tonight. They stopped in and asked me to join them . . . they tried to entice me by saying all the women were bringing a different-flavored cake. "Get a box of Betty Crocker and make one and bring it," they said. My dog was growling at them, so I couldn't open my door all the way to let them in. Besides, my life looks so suspicious and unreligious anymore that I cringe when they drop by. J.D. kept saying, "Make me some tea!" loudly in the background, which was like saying "God is dead" or something. Sometimes I think of rejoining them. At least our lives were cleaner then. There was an order to the chaos. There was a confined feeling. No coffee, no tea, no alcohol, no fighting, no swearing, no slothfulness, no thinking.

The Mormon women keep their houses clean, and the children clean, and they often dress in outfits that match their little scrubbed daughters. My children always look grubby no matter what I do. We creep out of our house to the car and make our way to the corner store. Nobody has brushed hair; no one has clean hands; our clothes are rumpled and slept-in looking; and I usually have soot on my face from sticking my head in the stove while trying to light it. But still, I feel more alive than when I was a Mormon. Somehow, when I was a Mormon all we ever did was clean up and go to church. We were always traveling toward the ward and the kids were always trying to sneak candy on fast and testimonial Sundays. There was nothing so embarrassing as the sound of my kids crunching next to me in the pew while someone stood in the front of the room and talked about how this day was a day to show God our love by not eating. But even then, come to think of it, I could never stick to a one-day fast. Iggy Stains, on the other hand, has a hard time eating. He is always finding a reason to fast.

"I didn't know whether to come visit 'cha without calling first, so I figured I better fast and pray and ask heavenly Father about it." This was one of the things I liked about Iggy . . . that he could go for long periods (like a camel) without eating or drinking. I admire that in a human.

Just yesterday while I was working at the Hurry Up grocery store, I saw an employee of Today & Yesterday food chain. I knew her when I had been active in the Mormon Church. She was standing in line reading *Misinfo!!,* the only tabloid we carry at Hurry Up. On the cover was Oprah Winfrey dressed in a red outfit with gold earrings . . . smiling to the camera, which meant she had lost weight. Oprah is our country's scale . . . if she is thin, we are thin or we at least begin dieting. If Oprah has gained, the feeling of "Oh who cares anymore" sweeps across the groceries like sagebrush through a ghost town (don't I sound like Zane Grey?) and the whole country gains with her. But the odd thing is that Oprah never looks any different to me. She is pretty when the tabloids say OPRAH GAINED IT ALL BACK!!! and still pretty when the papers say OPRAH'S NEWEST DIETING SECRET! AND LOOK HOW IT WORKS!!! and there will be Oprah, wearing a black dress or a little pink coat and a belt around her waist and she is smiling. This is disconcerting. What if dieting doesn't drastically change you? The readers sigh and pull in their stomachs . . . it's time to put away the fruitcake, the candy, the whatever and read how she did it.

"Well, hi, howreyadoing?" my Mormon friend Sissy asked, pushing her cereal boxes along the conveyor belt. She put the tabloid back in its rack while I rang up her groceries. I was thinking, "Gee, she's lost weight . . . all that fasting keeps Mormons thin" though I knew she had had a kidney infection at one point from fasting too much when her husband left her. When the Mormons fast, they don't drink any water . . . it is their way of suffering as Christ did in the desert. Sissy's husband left her for a redhead who had gone inactive, and she overfasted. She got a kidney infection after a few weeks and was hospitalized. She said she prayed the whole way in the ambulance, and her husband met her at the emergency room. He never strayed again . . . well, I can't say *never* because who knows? That didn't happen that long ago . . . anyway, she was in my checkout line buying Goofy Grape cereal and whole milk and a case of Campbell's soup and while I checked her through, she told me what was going on at the Today & Yesterday. "The manager, Mr. Marrow, fired three employees last week for being slow about spraying water over the vegetables . . . and my heck, one of them was his ex-wife." Sissy had a lot of coupons with her so I rang them in while I said, "He's divorced? I got a call from him once you know . . . I sort of thought he might be nice . . ."

She shook her head. "My heck, right before the holidays he fires his ex-wife . . . I mean what if they have children? I'm lucky Herb came home when he did or I'd be more worried about losing my job." She's always bringing up the fact that she got Herb back. Not that it's *wrong* but to me, a single, lonely, desperate, divorced woman, well, it's painful . . . why didn't *my* men come back?

I'll tell you why the father of Grace and J.D. didn't come back. Because he was a good Italian who did what his parents requested of him. And his parents didn't like me . . . why do the in-laws always play such a prominent part in the lives of young lovers? If only the Montagues and the Capulets had left Romeo and Juliet alone they might have had a long and desperately intense affair . . . or, on the other hand, they might have had twins and split up because the pressure of children is really intense. I'm not against procreating or anything; it's just that it seems to make the man lose interest. It tends to wreck the relationship.

Brandied Relationship Ring Flambé ⌗⌗⌗⌗⌗⌗⌗⌗⌗

Follow recipe for dark fruitcake and add to it 1 beautiful red-haired Italian man, one dark-haired woman, the thrust of desire, the seed of want, the milk of human kindness, spicy interludes, nutty remarks, juicy tidbits, and a variety of life. Pour into ring mold and as it begins to set, add 1 or more children . . . immediate separation will occur, at which point ladle in brandy and ignite.

"I challenge you to come to church this Sunday," Sissy was saying, as I bagged her groceries. "My heck we haven't seen you there in a long time . . . heavenly Father misses you. We all do."

"What about Mr. Marrow?" I asked. There was no one else in line behind her, so she put her brown bags down.

"He's there . . . at the store . . ."

"But is he hiring again? Why did he fire three people?" I was trying to sound casual but a hint of hysteria was creeping into my voice. I sounded like my mother when she didn't know where one of us was. "I mean . . . is he needing somebody?"

"Gosh, I don't know," Sissy said. "I think he let

those folks go because there isn't enough work to hold on to all the employees. Aren't you happy here?" Suddenly I saw her looking deeply at me and I was filled with shame. Beyond my drab checkout apron and my Hurry Up hat, beyond my wild unkempt hair that never stayed in place, beyond all the obvious faults, I saw what my Mormon friend saw . . . a roving lost soul, teetering on the wicked . . . seesawing toward evildoing by lusting after that which she did not have. "Thou shalt not covet thy neighbor's wife, nor thy neighbor's ass nor oxen . . ." I suppose that also means thou shalt not covet any man but wait ye therefore instead and either one will come along or one won't . . . but quit coveting. I felt terrible guilt and humiliation then, looking at my clean, tidy, friendly Mormon friend. Why couldn't I be like that? . . . tidy and married and shopping for cereal?

After she left, I closed my aisle briefly and went to the coffee room where I looked up the phone number of Mr. Marrow and dialed it directly from the pay phone. When he answered his voice terrified me. "Hello," he said. I couldn't respond so I hung up.

All cookbooks should have some recipes that nobody would ever in a million years go near. Like goose liver on porcupine thighs. So I will insert one here.

Foie Gras—Soft Butt End with Musk Glands in Foil

Immediately after killing, remove skin from flesh and soak separately in brine. If animal was trapped, meat will be less soft. If animal was scared out of its wits, it will be rock hard. Dip in seasoned flour and cultured cream. Cook fatty side up at 300° till done. May be wrapped in foil as long as the foil has had seasoning corrected. Remove claws before eating.

Bon appetit!

Funny how peoples' names often lead them into their line of work. Like the doctor who delivered Shelley was named Dr. Cockanhour and here was Mr. Marrow, working behind the butchered meats . . .

The part of me consumed by rage is diverted. My hatred and fury spill into everything. The fire insurance people who have canceled my policy for some unknown reason . . . stating "outer structure of dwelling unkempt." I imagine scenarios where I become an excellent risk and snootily go to another company while my old company stands by, ashamed.

My rage spills over onto the man who is suing me for a nine-dollar bounced check. Yes, I wrote the check; no, I didn't know the account had been closed by the disapproving bank that was tired of charging me check-bouncing fees. Yes, I tried to repay the creepy man; no, he wouldn't accept the nine dollars or even the fifty-six dollars I tried to give him. He wants one hundred dollars, in cash, in small bills. I hate him. I wish he would suddenly get down on his knees and say, "God, how wicked I have been! I will forgive this insignificant woman her bad check and, yea, I will even embrace her poverty and offer her a job checking at my store."

Rage permeates the house. I yell at the children and refuse to pat the dog. *Rage!* Because, you see, the world has gone to war.

Decorating and remodeling your home: high ceilings and glass accessories give this living room a bright and cheerful look while the brocade sofa offers warmth. The antique brick fireplace, saved from the original dwelling, is an inviting place to entertain, with overstuffed chairs surrounding the hearth. Indian artifacts on the wall are from the owner's private collection, picked up on various trips to reservations in New Mexico. For information on furnishings, turn to page 88.

I'm angry that the dentist charged me ninety dollars to fill two of Grace's little cavities. Little seven-year-old Grace! I hate them all. I hate everything.

"At this point in time, we think we have hit some

or most of the Iraqi scud missile sites, but we . . . uh . . . can't at this time say with all accuracy exactly *which* ones or what, if any, are left . . . uh . . . until more data and information come to us from the Gulf."

There is another part of me that is not at all filled with rage. It is decimated with fear. I am sure that everything is going to fall completely to pieces; all my quilts will be ruined; the children will . . . well, let's just say I'm frightened. *The world is frightened! Iraq bombs Israel!* Bush condemns scud missile attack on Israel.

There was a peace march in town one night, and I stood with some people on a patch of park area. They said, "Would you like a sign to hold?" but I said no because I do not know what I want or feel. I know I am frightened. "Would you like a yellow ribbon to wear?" they said. I took one, but I just held it in my hand. It seemed to be so insignificant. What would this tiny ribbon with blurred words on it do? This was no match for missiles. Human beings are diminished in the face of this warfare.

Although I am frozen silent by the war and have nothing really to say, I will say something. As I was driving home after taking J.D. to his Big Brother's college room (they get together on Sundays and watch TV) I stopped to buy milk. In the store I saw newspapers and on the front page of one was a picture of a long-legged, long-necked bird covered in black oil. It conveyed everything of the war in its eyes that stared right at the photographer. The same look as the Jews in the Nazi camp pictures. Outside my window is an enormous mountain of filthy snow that the town dumps here when the streets are snowy. They pile it in one huge mountain all around an ancient walnut tree in the cow field. Last year the walnut tree quit bearing walnuts. I have nothing to say. I want to scream at officials and cry to the populations but I am silenced by myself. I imagine we are all silenced. Some people say, "Support our men in the Gulf" or "Support our *boys* in the Gulf" and some people say, "Stop the war *now*" and some people say, "I don't know what to think" and some people say "Saddam Hussein is a crazy Hitler and I support President Bush in his decision" and some people, like me, say nothing. When I saw the photograph of the bird standing by the black oil ocean, covered in oil, I sucked in my breath so loudly it sounded like a scream. There were two guys in the store, flirting with the girl behind the counter. "Well, have a nice breakfast," she said.

"What do you want us to bring you from McDonald's?" one guy asked her.

She laughed. "Nothin'," she said.

"Aw, come on . . . hash browns? Let's see . . . two hash browns and a cup of coffee," he persisted.

Meanwhile, I was approaching the counter, unable to contain myself. "Oh, God, God," I said to Grace, who was with me. "It's so terrible . . ."

"I can make myself something here," she said.

"I wanna get you somethin'," the guy said.

I'll say one thing. The war in the Persian Gulf has brought the species closer again instantly. Not *all* men and women are responding so quickly to each other . . . but enough are . . . and I can feel the difference on the street. In the voices of women on the radio: "I mean, jeez . . . why can't we just support our guys and . . . and let the leaders of the countries decide if it's right or not? I mean, they're already over there . . . why hurt their morale?"

We see pictures of young men sitting on sand dunes, shaving, surrounded by sandbags. We see them in heavy gear and wearing masks to keep out poison. We hear they will be watching the Super Bowl Monday night and eating chips and dip but drinking near-beer because of the religion in Saudi Arabia. I can imagine the men there and how uncomfortable it is and how scary to hear the bombs and the shooting. How thrilling it is. How horrifying. But we don't get to see the Iraqi people at all.

I was in Saudi Arabia once, wasn't I? No, just in Syria. But it is like saying you were in Texas but never in Massachusetts. They are all brother countries there as we are all Americans. They are also similar . . . The two guys who were flirting with the girl didn't buy a paper. They only came in to flirt.

I have nothing to say, nothing to say, nothing to say.

"You hear about the house that burned down last night?" Hester asked me on the phone. "Burnt right to the ground. Not a stick left. We heard it come over the scanner. I woke up 'cause, you know . . . the scanner will be quiet for a while and then *all of a sudden* it gets like that, you know . . . real loud. Woke me right up."

I was quilting on an Amish lone star and saying "Huh!" every so often into the mouthpiece.

"Hey-yep," Hester went on, "this morning I guess it was still burning. I feel bad for the folks that lived in it. Apparently they was still in their nighties when they made a run for it to the neighbors."

"What do you think about the war?" I said.

"I think it's plain stupid, that's what. I don't like war. And I didn't vote for that man Bush, neither. It's a big waste," she said.

Now instead of the world slowing down on its axis, I am afraid a big black cloud will cover the sky. I am fearful of going outside now because I imagine a darkness arriving, of looking up and seeing it is the horror from the Middle East come, the soot falling everywhere, the black cloud obliterating the sun. The smell of oil and filth. I am afraid to turn on the water faucet for fear of black sludge pouring out . . . so this is the way we will go!

"Just when we thought it was all over with Russia," Hester said, "and now this." We sighed into the phone. "Stop down," she said.

"Yeah," I said. "I will when I get a minute . . ." but I secretly thought I wouldn't stop down . . . that I would stay in my house forever and hide. Let the bills pile up and people think I was a lunatic. I would shut the world out.

"In the news this morning, Saddam Hussein said he would now begin using an *unconventional* weapon." I am half listening to the radio and trying to get the fire started with wet wood. J.D. is at his Big Brother's . . . that's a nice program for children without fathers. ". . . shot down two scuds during an all-night . . ." Grace is in the hallway, drawing and making Valentines. Even the newspaper is wet. ". . . the Bills and the Patriots tonight in an all- . . ." I am suddenly confused. I feel foggy and lost, as if I have just crawled out of bed in the middle of the night. I feel like a dumb steer being herded somewhere. Did the man on the radio say something about the football game or was it the Patriot missile he was referring to? I bump into the stove. My hands are black from soot, the fire smokes and I cannot get that pathetic bird out of my head. ". . . thirty miles or more of black crude along the coast of . . ." I am flying up toward the ceiling, rushing, trying to get God's attention, trying to respond. The Earth rumbles through me. I think all species must be feeling this similar yank. Like the sameness in the Arabs, in the United States, all living species must also be enough alike to hear the silent death of part of our nation.

In an argument about whether to stop the war over Helen of Troy: "Nay, if we talk of reason, / Let's shut our gates, and sleep." So it was said to Priam and Hector in *Troilus and Cressida*. Shakespeare knew the rub. Let us shut up our gates and sleep. Let the little bandy-legged birds in Persia live. Let us shut up our gates and sleep.

The personal ads have been disappearing and instead come angry letters over the crisis in the Persian Gulf.

> I can't understand these flag-burning peaceniks. Don't they realize this is a free country where they don't get arrested for having their own opinion? And it's our young men and women who are over there in Saudi Arabia defending that freedom. Seems like they could do something more productive and help out our boys. I think people who burn flags ought to be shot for treason.

"Cry, Trojans, cry! . . . Cry, Trojans, cry!" (Cassandra, in *Troilus and Cressida*.) You know Cassandra . . . she was the daughter of Priam who knew everything that was going to happen in the future, but nobody believed her. That is the worst imaginable—to know of the horror to come and have no one believe you.

The head of the conservation and environment in Saudi Arabia was on the radio yesterday. He sounded awfully upset. "Thees eez the worst oil sleek disaster een history," I think he said. Maybe somebody else said that. Anyway, the Saudi Arabian was devastated. And they are a difficult bunch to get upset when it comes to environmental issues.

"Cry, Trojans, cry!" But they said, "Oh, don't pay any attention to Cassandra. She's mad." "Poor thing," they said. "Completely crazy. Hector, die? What a nut."

Today I got up my courage and went back to the Diet Center. Many diet centers around the country are having a hard time financially. This is the last one left in Vermont. My counselor gave me a cursory once-over glance and noted I had put on weight. I can tell she is doing that. Then she says, "Well, how was your weekend?" and I say, "You mean after the Ben and Jerry's truckload sale or before?" and she says, "Oooooh, why did you do that?" She looks at me with great concern but, hey, who are we kidding? We both know *why* I did that. It's just a matter now of "can I quit momentarily or am I off and running for another ten pounds?"

"Why? Well, uh, I guess, the war made me do it," I

say. She looks at me, a peculiar expression on her face. I can't describe it.

"Well, I went to a religious ceremony on Saturday," she says. "It was really interesting and peaceful. We believe there is a positive force in nature and good can come from it."

I nod. I guess I am too negative. "I guess I'm too negative," I say. "But that poor bird on the front page of the paper . . . and the terrible destruction going on over there . . ."

"So you decided to destroy your diet along with all that?" she says, half laughing, half chiding. "Good, Gabby, good."

She weighs me. It turns out not to be so bad. Only one pound. But I feel enormous, as though everything in the world was sitting inside my stomach, weighing me down to the floor, through the floor into the ground, straight to the molten center and right out the other side.

"My life could have been a lot worse," my counselor says. "And yours could too. I mean, think of the people who have been victims of incest!" I think, and it fills me with sorrow.

"God," I say. "It's so sad. It's so awful." I could cry, thinking about it.

I realize I have brought my counselor down during our talk. I am full of gloomy, lumpy sorrow and Ben & Jerry's ice cream. Maybe it's *me* I am pitying. Last night, when I was trying to get a log out of the icy ground to put in the stove, I looked up at the moon and it had the face of a woman. I always thought the moon was a man, but I see now she is a woman . . . and she was looking rather complacent. I tried to see her as devastated or even as a corpse, but she would not change her expression, no matter how I blurred my eyes. She looked merely complacent, and she was looking right at me. Suddenly my legs slipped out from under me and I was in a kneeling position on the icy ground.

"Whoa!" I thought. "If I'm not careful I'm liable to crack up completely!" I got up and hustled into the house and spent the evening listening to the lousy reception on the radio. J.D. and Grace sat with me at the country kitchen table and we played Go Fish over and over. It got to be very funny, because no matter how much we shuffled the cards Grace kept winning almost on her first turn.

"Do you have a ten?" she'd say to me.

"Augh!" I said.

"Do you have a three?"

"Augh!" I said.

"Do you have a nine?"

"Augh!" I said.

"I'm out. I win."

"Augh!" J.D. said. Then we all laughed hysterically.

"Good evening, this is NPR news," and I quit playing.

War Waffles ¤¤¤¤¤¤¤¤¤¤¤¤¤¤¤¤¤¤¤¤¤¤¤¤¤¤¤¤¤¤

This recipe is for the hearty iron stomachs in your family—or it can be used as a table game.

1. Big countries, big weapons
2. A good cause
3. Flat pan to wage batter in and lay out strategy
4. 1 or more victims
5. Heroes, villains and neutral patties
6. Compassion fruit (omitted from syrup)

Pan is heated when you start. Pour batter directly onto heat and close lid of waffle iron. When everything comes out in neat little squares, stack on top of neutral patties and pour on the syrup. Whichever waffle is the most syrup-soaked wins the plate war.

To make the syrup: add warheads to water. Let bleed through colander and pack into cavity of syrup bottle. Shoot onto waffles; withhold compassion fruit.

A few days ago this acquaintance of mine who had a vasectomy back when it was the *in* thing to do (his wife left him after that and he put on ninety pounds) saw me in the health food store.

"Well, well, well," he said, "and are we living with somebody?"

I was holding a loaf of French bread, which I was tapping against my arm.

"Not me," I said. "I wish I was," I added.

"Hard to believe," he went on, licking his large lips and staring at me. "You're not a bad piece of real estate."

"Thank you," I said. I was so shocked I didn't know what to say. And now that I think of it, maybe that isn't what he meant at all . . . maybe we were talking about where I live. Yes, I think we were . . . and maybe that's when he said "not a bad piece of real estate." Maybe he wasn't referring to me . . . but after that I left the store thinking, "Men love football and men love war and men love real estate. Jesus," and I went home with a pint of ice cream and a jar of Hershey chocolate sauce and I thought, "Boy, am I glad I'm not with a man." After all, this war will take another toll on our American men and even fewer of us will have a chance at marriage or love. Probably it will be more likely that Joan Rivers will go to Pluto than a single woman will find a man.

Cry, Trojans, cry!

Oh, what a longing for a man! A man who comes into a room, commands the eyes of every person . . . strong legs, lean eyes (romance writers call them "hungry" eyes), a chest that would make a woman swoon to put her head on . . . any sort of man. A garbage collecting man. A soldier. Horrible to say, but when listening to reports of our brave soldiers in the Gulf I can't help being attracted to them. Their soldier suits are so appealing. Well, not the older generals who stand in front of maps on TV and point to where the army is . . . they wear pajamalike camouflage shirts and pants, loose over their bellies. They remind me of a chubby cousin of mine who plays plastic army before going to bed at night. They stand there and say, "Oh, no . . . I won't tell you *that*! That's giving away secrets!" But the sexy whispering of the army scout on the midday report, softly saying, "I'll go in here and check over the terrain . . . make sure the troops can come in without problems . . . I usually carry just a rifle and that's all . . ." and the whispered response from the follow-up unit, "Keep an eye on him . . . make sure no one bothers him . . . I can blow up this whole area in five minutes, sir."

This is all very exciting, and I think it isn't just me who gets charged from these intimate, dangerous conversations in the black desert night. Of course, being dead isn't sexy, but usually the news doesn't dwell on the dead people. They dwell on the sexy, powerful *living*.

"How old are you?" the newsman asks the army scout.

"I'm twenty, sir," the scout whispers. And then he sort of laughs under his breath, like when you are in bed with someone and you're nervous, but it's good, too.

This morning Shelley said to me, as she swung her backpack over one shoulder and headed off to school in her C.B. sportswear, "You're gaining weight again, Mom."

And so I am. I sit glued to the radio, eating Fritos, ice cream and doughnuts while listening to the news.

"It's my stomach, isn't it?" I asked.

"No," Shelley said, grabbing an apple (she is *so* virtuous in comparison to her fat mother!), "it's your face. Your eyes aren't so big anymore. Well, bye!"

Grace was sitting at the country kitchen table on a ladderback chair that belonged to my great-great grandmother.

"I don't think you're fat," she offered. "But you smell like coffee when you kiss me. Eeeew."

I decided to call my Diet Center counselor. Of course, I know the number by heart, just as I know the number of the police station, the children's school, the number of the grocery where I used to work.

"I've lost control again," I said when she picked up the phone. "I've been overeating for two weeks. I don't deny myself *anything.*"

"I cried all the way to work," she said to me. "So we're both doing what we feel like doing . . . and that's okay but now we should find another means of expressing ourselves. Today you will eat healthy!"

"Today I will eat healthy," I repeated. "Why did you cry on the way to work?"

My Diet Center counselor laughed. "Oh, well, I

don't know. I didn't want to come in, that's all. My husband said, 'Hey, you're a good Christian woman . . . God-fearing . . . find the answer in prayer.' He was right." My counselor always makes me feel better.

"I'm really going to pull it together today," I said. But even though I used to be a Mormon, I find no comfort in praying to God. Sometimes I feel the Earth speaks to me and the sky speaks to me, and perhaps even God is relaying messages, but when I fold my hands and say, "Please, God, help me not eat junk food," nothing happens. Nothing at all.

I don't mean to be anti-American, but I bet the Iraqi soldiers are sexy too. Except yesterday there was a report about their having head lice. Head lice is not sexy. Head lice and death. I should make a list of what to avoid in a soldier. Head lice, death, pajamas.

In *Troilus and Cressida,* they call war with Troy a "sport." Actually, Troilus says, "But to the sport abroad. Are you bound thither?" Which means, "Aren't you coming to the sport?" And while the men go to the field for the sport, women (Helen and Cressida, etc.) watch from their towers. "They go to their towers to watch," and so the war in the Persian Gulf is laid out. The men go to the bloody sport, and they even liken it to football terms and basketball talk:

"The ball's in Saddam's court," a general said. But the women have to stay home and watch on their TVs or listen to the radio instead of getting tower seats. Times change.

My quilt teacher said once, "Gabby, we have to find you somebody nice and stable . . . somebody who won't run away. You have the worst luck with men who run off . . ." Secretly, this nice remark made me feel terrible. I'm not so sure I have bad luck . . . maybe I drive these fellows away with a stick . . . "That's providing you want a husband and sometimes they're more trouble than they're worth," my quilt teacher went on, and the other married women in the quilt class agreed . . . but it was that cozy "we don't really mean it" sort of agreement. They were clucking over their good luck. I'm always the pathetic ugly duckling in my quilt class. Even my quilts come out divorced from the group. While the other students make even straight seams that all meet in a pleasing trip around the world or a flying geese pattern, my lone star or my log cabin slides out of my sewing machine and bunches and warps. "She doesn't know what an iron is" my quilt teacher explains when some bystander looks politely at my quilt. My quilt teacher will admit that my quilts have a lot of color. But she adds with a secret smile that my colors may all end up brown after a single wash because I don't wash my material beforehand. It is the way I view life. I risk the bleeding.

Hester makes her quilts like I do . . . only she doesn't go out and buy her material . . . she cuts up old clothes and though I may have an Olfa cutter and a green mat board and polyester 100 percent quilting thread and Gingher scissors, Hester makes the real McCoy. She's the pioneer around here.

"If you'd learn to pin correctly, Gabby, you'd have some *beautiful* quilts . . . your hand quilting is good, but you have to remember to stitch *where the pin goes in*! And you have to find yourself a husband." My quilt teacher is right. The pinning is important. But I'm worried that I am too hard on husbands.

Hester and I took a walk in the balmy February thaw last night.

"I'm working on my log cabin quilt," she said. "I've put one square together to see how it'll look."

I was thinking, "Well, here I am, exercising, finally. Maybe I can lose some weight tonight," and aloud I said, "I'm working on my Amish lone star for Grace. I have it nearly all quilted."

Hester waved her flashlight around in the darkness. "Did you hear those chain saws today?" she asked me. "I was busy makin' a pie so I didn't go out to see, but I heard 'em sawing all day."

"They were cutting down the dead trees where the

birds roost," I said. "The birds were screaming and carrying on so much I felt like calling the Audubon Society . . . but I didn't. I just let it go. I never fight back."

"Well, I knew they were doing something," she said. She played the light of the flashlight around on the hill, but we could see nothing.

"Muddy out," she said. It was an awkward walk. We hadn't been out walking for almost a month and so we suddenly had nothing to say. On top of the hill a figure appeared, and Hester said, "There's my daughter."

I called out hello and turned back toward my house.

"I have to put the kids to bed," I said. But when I got home the kids were making a restaurant in Grace's room and Shelley was washing her whites in bleach.

"Is this too much bleach?" she wanted to know. I watched her load the machine and then went to bed with an old Nancy Drew book. Nancy Drew always had such an easy life. There was never any war going on and the worst thing that happened to her was she got thrown into a closet with a gag in her mouth, which she wiggled out of, and occasionally someone smashed her car and told her to stay out of their business. Mostly, though, she nibbled on Hannah Gruen's yummy food and danced with Ned Nickerson. Things came easily to her . . . mysteries and friends, vacations and money. How did she get all that money to drive around solving mysteries? What did Carson Drew ever do? He was a noted lawyer, so say the books, but he never was able to solve anything without Nancy's getting thrown into a closet or being locked in a hidden drawer or something. Nancy's mother was dead, so there was nobody to say, "Nancy, quit fooling around with dangerous people and get your own apartment." Nancy Drew was so lucky. I never liked the descriptions of her, though . . . slim, with blond hair, with dresses and pumps. She sounded like a secretary instead of a wild daredevil. I would rather have had her dark-haired with jeans and sweaters in a Volkswagen. But the image of a "low-slung roadster" was, I guess, more mysterious because no one knows what that is.

Dear Iggy Stains:

Were you called away to serve your country? I haven't heard from you in ages. Was it your awkward visit to my house last fall that severed our ties? I heard on the news that a soldier from Bountiful, Utah, died in the war, shot perhaps by FRIENDLY FIRE. I learned that friendly fire is when an American gets killed by mistake by another American. I also heard on the news that there have been six suicides in the Persian Gulf troops since the war broke out, or since they were stationed there. Do you suppose they killed themselves because they were frightened? Or do you think (as the news suggested) that they were depressed and lonely away from their families?

Let me say, Iggy, that I cannot marry you because I am no longer a good Mormon. I never go to church, and I drink coffee every morning. I swear at my children when I get mad, and I don't think God is waiting for me to baptize my dead relatives.

I DO believe in love and kindness and the Ten Commandments. And I believe that anyone who was like Jesus should be honored and adored. I believe that God is good and just, but I think he would be understanding too. I can't believe that the wars with the Nephites and the Laminites (in the Book of Mormon) are something we are all supposed to study and pray over. Maybe some of us are supposed to do that, but I think others are supposed to do other things . . . we can't all be supposed to do the same thing here on Earth . . . it would be a waste. Too repetitive, don't you think? Maybe some of us are supposed to baptize dead people and others are supposed to preach and others are supposed to sing and others to learn languages and some to dig up gold plates and some not to. The chances are, though, that I am wrong and you are right. You have more on your side than me.

Also, I couldn't marry you because you are so fearful and rigid in a way that baffles me. Why would you be afraid to take an art class and work from a nude model? Why does that seem dirty to you? Anyway, if you are being called away to active duty in the Gulf, I will marry you just to serve my country, but don't expect me to live in Bountiful, Utah, if you return. I am an East Coast girl at heart and couldn't bear to leave the north-east region . . .

Best,
Gabby Fulbriten

Hester's husband has developed cancer. She stays at home now and they sit in their living room listening to the television. Sometimes when I visit she gives me tea and cookies but often she is not there . . . They go to the doctor's a lot. Because he is so ill, sometimes I drive them to the doctor's and while he is being examined, Hester and I talk about quilts and long winters and how her husband is doing . . . we can't talk much when he is around because he is bored and he likes to be in on the conversation and when he is, it just isn't the same. He doesn't quilt or sympathize with wildlife . . . he doesn't know any recipes. "I didn't make my fruitcakes this year," I said, sitting with Hester in the doctor's office. We weren't the only people in the waiting room . . . there were a few sad-looking women waiting to see the doctor. He was a cancer specialist.

"No, me neither," Hester said. "I did my fudge and

my peanut brittle. I like a little peanut brittle during the cold months . . . and some banana breads . . . and I made my chocolate candies . . . and that's *it*! I'm not making anything else; they'll just have to make do with what they get." She laughed and threw her hands into her lap . . . "I wish I'd brought my sewing with me," she said, looking at my sewing. I was working on an appliqué square.

"Isn't this pretty?" I said, holding it up. The two other women in the room lifted their eyes to glance at the square.

"My mother used to appliqué," one woman said. "She made all the quilts in our home and some of them are on display now . . ."

"Why don't you sell some of those and make yourself some money? Gee . . . you could use the income . . . those are nice enough to sell." Hester took the square from me and examined it. "Plenty would buy those," she said and handed it back to me.

"Oh . . . I couldn't get the money back that I put into them," I said.

The woman across the room looked up again. "That's right . . . my mother said the quilting business was in the hands of the Chinese and the people in Thailand. They are producing them in factories hand made for a fraction of the cost it takes in the States . . . my mother told me that . . . she's dead now but she made many beautiful things."

Hester shifted in her plastic seat. It always makes

Hester uncomfortable to talk about people dying of cancer. "Well, I say sell a few. Make yourself some spending money. I always called it pocket money. That's the money I set aside to spend on whatever. Pocket money." Hester kept her hands in her lap and waited for her husband to come out of the examining room.

The option to marry Iggy remains in the back of my mind. If and when the bills get too high, the winters get too rough, the loneliness gets too overwhelming, *then* I will send for Iggy. It is as if he was a mail-order husband . . . available through the Sears, Roebuck catalog. IGGY STAINS COMPLETE WITH MARITAL BED MADE OF SOLID OAK COVERED IN WHITE LINENS FROM IRELAND . . . SEND $6.40 NOW! I say Ireland because I have been doing a little research on *husband material.* I have oft pretended that I would find where they are and fly hence . . . unto their outstretched arms. (Feeling desperate and getting poetic go hand in hand with me.) Anyway, I decided to find out if there were men on other continents . . . if there were men available, indeed, anywhere. Taking out my maps and my statistics, I reasoned there would be older, single, available men in countries where the women were allowed to emigrate . . . and there would be men willing to relocate in places where times were difficult. Not the Middle East because the men were too dangerous.

Not Europe because there were too many beautiful women there. Not Mexico because there was too much dysentery and stuff that would hamper a romantic holiday. No, it had to be a place where the country was torn by trouble, where the men spoke my language, where the women weren't as desperate as America . . . I came upon Belfast, Ireland, and immediately procured brochures to browse through. I came up with an idea—while I was gone, Shelley would stay with her dad and the twins would live at my mother's. I would come back with a cute Irish husband whom I would have to protect from the other single American women lurking everywhere and we would have a happy Irish life planting potatoes by the old stump dump. After all, back at the turn of the century, men went off and gathered an unknown foreign wife and brought her to Alaska with them. It's common knowledge there were ads in the papers needing wives.

Man-made Potato Soup ¤¤¤¤¤¤¤¤¤¤¤¤¤¤¤¤¤¤

Potatoes	***Water***
Onions	***Milk***
Blender	

Put potatoes and other ingredients in blender. Have man turn blender on to high. Have man pour liquid into saucepan and heat over flame till bubbly.

Pour into bowls and eat with man. Clean up after you make love on rug.

> *Alas, alas, I must away*
> *to Ireland at break of*
> *day*
> *to find a male*
> *before I'm bent and*
> *gray!!*

But when it comes down to purchasing the ticket, of course, I am stumped. Perhaps I could marry Iggy and convince him to take me to Ireland where he could fall in a bog and I could then proceed with my plan. I have read much about these *bogs.* They are cold and deep and you happen upon them without warning when you are out walking in the hills of Ireland . . . not too terribly long ago a six hundred-year-old woman was found in one of these *bogs* and she was in perfect condition . . . dead, but still wearing her little leather shoes and still contained in her own skin. Because the *bogs* are like big freezers . . . cold deep dark water. Working at the Hurry Up grocery, it would take me *years* to save enough for a ticket to go . . . plus the brochures on Ireland say it is best to have your own vehicle to travel in because there aren't trains over there . . . and I'd need a new wardrobe . . . no, the option to marry Iggy is more probable. I'll sit down tonight and write him a suggestive letter . . . I'll tell him I'm ready to be humbled. I'll quit coffee and allow him to lead me through life, a blind and patient wife, meek, quiet, dressed in demure colors and modest clothing. Our home will have consistency . . . like pudding.

Iggy Pudding ¤¤¤¤¤¤¤¤¤¤¤¤¤¤¤¤¤¤¤¤¤¤¤¤¤¤¤¤¤

If you have a man as an option, marry him. There is no greater consistency than a predictable man. Once married, bubbles can be smoothed out as you stir. Some lumps are desirable . . . Do not overmix! Serve Iggy pudding with a cup of good cheer . . . (nonalcoholic) (we won't go until we get some we won't go until we get some we won't go until we get some we won't go until we get some, so bring it right here . . . etc.)

Because Hester's husband is so ill now, going over to her house to sew is stilted. Our conversation centers around whether or not his Cat scan came back and when his next trip for therapy is . . . Sometimes I feel more lonely after I've visited . . . She is my best friend but her best friend is her husband and he's very ill. So we don't laugh as much. When I say silly things she looks at me with a severe look. Not always . . . but enough to shut me up. "I struggled raising my kids alone like you," she has said on many occasions to me. "My husband was in the forces and he was gone a lot

. . . and I raised my children alone. And I know what you mean when you say it's hard . . . but . . ." she raises her hands in surrender ". . . you do what you have to do. You *make* do. I remember there were times I took in wash to make ends meet." Hester's wisdom follows me everywhere. Imagine taking in wash! I don't even do my own . . . and anyway, people don't do that anymore, do they? I mean, there are fancy machines that wash and dry. "When I needed money for something extra . . . why I just had to scrape together what was there . . . no bank would give me a loan 'cause I was a woman and banks didn't give loans to women . . . nope. I raised my kids and kept my home and paid my bills same as everybody else. But it was hard. I know that much." Having Hester's husband be so ill is like losing Hester. Once she had me drive her to the pharmacy for some personal items for him, and while she went through the aisles looking for things, I waited by the cash register. "May I help you?" the pharmacist said. "No," I said. "I'm just waiting." Always waiting, never finding . . . that's me I guess. While my friend tended to her husband's needs, the clock ticked away. On the way home, Hester said something to me that she's said before . . . "Gabby, you're better off than you think—least you have a roof over your head—might leak some, but it's yours." We laughed briefly. When I dropped her off, she gave me a sack of newspapers to burn. "He can't see well enough to read them anymore," she said, referring to her husband. "And he won't eat much—no point in cooking just for me." I took the newspapers and drove home. The kids had gotten off the school bus and were fighting over the sled.

As I sit quilting on my sampler quilt, I listen to *Twelfth Night* on cassette. There is much laughing and jovial behavior in *Twelfth Night* by Shakespeare. The servants gang up on a pompous servingman of the lady of the house and make a great fool of him . . . they snicker through many scenes as I stitch. But I cannot find the humor in it today. I have been thinking instead of the hundreds of mothers and babies who were incinerated last night during an air raid in Iraq. I have been thinking how people in Leadbelly wear yellow ribbons and flag pins in support of the troops . . . and how slowly it comes over me that it seems a kind of support of butchery. I know it is un-American to not support the war, but I do not like this war. I do not. It rings of all the bad things this country has done in the past. Hiroshima and Nagasaki and Vietnam. We are too powerful to be killing those children. The news said the fathers of the dead children babbled incoherently at the bomb shelter where hundreds of burned bodies lay. They screamed and sobbed and beat their heads upon the ground.

There is an article in the paper calling one journalist in the Gulf "scud stud" because he is handsome and divorced and tells us nightly of the scud attacks. There is another article I read while making a fire this morning about the Patriot football team making a dirty joke about the patriot missile and the Patriot football teams' "private parts." I would say the word "penis" but it might shock people.

I feel as weary as the Earth might feel. I feel as dull as the ground after thousands of sortie runs across a desert. I am as heavy as a cluster bomb and as hollow as a crater left by a missile. After you hear so much, you fall silent and no amount of horror can revive you . . . no amount of "think positive" can rally your brain. Because if you think, it will be of what you have heard, and it becomes too terrible and too incomprehensible to bear. It is like how Henry the Fifth felt when he discovered his bedfellow plotting with the French against him. Or like how Troilus felt when he watched Cressida flirting heavily with Diomedes. Troilus asked, after he saw it, "Was Cressida here? Was it real?" (I paraphrase), because horrible happenings give us an instant sort of amnesia to keep us from going mad. And so I, too, forget. I forget now that I was looking for a lover . . . a husband . . . a mate. I forget that going to McDonald's is like supporting Styrofoam. I forget a lot of things, so when I begin, for no reason, to cry as I stitch up one side of the sampler quilt and down the other, I wonder why, indeed, am I crying? *Am* I mad or is it possible that by a vote in heaven I have been chosen the new town crier? Am I not Gabby Fulbriten? Is this shabby house not my house by the dump? Are not my children all in school and eating lunch about now? Do I not make quilts and work in a grocery store? Or am I new, transformed? Call me not Gabby, I say! Today I will be Cassandra of Leadbelly!

I guess heavy doses of war news and Shakespeare have made me crack up. I think in war toy terms. "What's the game plan for today?" I muse, "After an attack on the fridge, I think I'll make the bunker beds and bomb out of here." Then, too, I think in olde English, like a Shakespeare play. "How doth the game plan for today, Lady?" I ask myself. "Beyond an attack upon the refrigerator, methinks it is kind of a blot to leave the bunker beds undone, and so I shall. A plague upon bedmaking, but not upon the making on a bed! What's that? What's that? Shall I not bomb out of here? Scurvy homemaker!"

What a narrow-minded little town this is! It comes over me as I drive home from the corner grocery, ripping open a bag of Fritos as I turn onto my street. It is boring and closed. I pass the town square, where a guy who once slept with me and dumped me, is sitting on a park bench, looking as handsome as that night. A lawyer's son whom I have since learned just hangs around his father's office picking up chicks. Do you mind that I call us "chicks"? We are, aren't we? "All my pretty ones?" . . . asks McDuff when he hears that his wife and children were slaughtered. "Did you say all? Oh, Hellkite! All? / What, all my pretty chickens . . . ?" Well, here we are but chicks against these slanderers who use our beds as parking spaces and never pay the toll. This dumb town . . . McDuff would have hated it here; everyone in Macbeth would have hated it here. No kings, no thanes, no spicy women, no witches; nay, no spot here. Just the UPS man when I pull into my street, driving ahead of me, as he always does; going toward my neighbor's house, as he always does. No, he is not having an affair—that would be too spicy, too rich for this town's blood. He is delivering another free gift. My neighbor sends away for every free or almost-free gift that is ever advertised on the side of cereal boxes. She saves coupons and redeems them through the mail for a variety of prizes, all delivered by the UPS man. I swing around him as he pulls into her drive, and when I get to my own dooryard I feel partially dead and partially revived enough to run away. This is ever my dilemma. To go! To go! Sell all and leave! My front door opens miraculously . . . as if by magic it is agreeing with me . . . but then . . .

"Mommy's home! Hurray, she got groceries! Hurray, she got Fritos! Look, she's eating Fritos! Hurray!" and, thud! the magic dissipates, dissolves, and I am but a drab woman who is fat from Fritos again. Nothing more, nothing less. Nothing of any note . . .

just what I am, bound in this dreary village to my off-spring.

Except there is one thing out of the ordinary in this odiously ordinary place, and that is that we have a wolf that walks right by our house every few days. At first it would walk along the ridge overlooking the new condo site. It was lean and hungry, like Cassius in *Julius Caesar*, looking to better itself with fresh flesh. It appeared to have mange. I never mentioned it because I was afraid Hester's husband might shoot it or trap it. I liked the idea of wildlife still existing around my house.

But then it moved closer. It is brazen as well, taking not a quiet wooded path to its destination, but padding right up the middle of the road and weaving off into the old town dump. Yesterday it stopped right outside my kitchen window. I was washing dishes and feeling ordinary and fat when I saw the huge reddish-gold wolf standing on the edge of my yard. He was gazing into the distance. His tail was puffed out to the size of our dog, and its body was enormous and almost catlike. A thrill of terror shot through me . . . here was danger, right outside my kitchen window . . . maybe I couldn't be Rosalind in *As You Like It* and dress up as a boy and get a duke's son to love me in the woods, but I could stand at my window and watch a wolf watching something. I followed his gaze, if you will (as

Nancy Drew often says) and lo, there was Grace in a bright red coat, climbing the filthy pile of snow that the town trucks dump in the pasture by our house. She was calling to her brother, J.D., and the wolf stared at them, motionless, like our cat stares, motionless, when a mole dares cross our yard. My hands were white with suds. I leaped to the door and went out, yelling to Grace, "Get off the snow! Get off! Come here! I said come here!"

The wolf didn't bother to look at me. He slid easily into the woods down by the dump. But Grace would not come. She danced on the oily snow pile and continued on her journey to cross it entirely.

"Grace! Come here, Grace!" I shouted.

But my children are not model children . . . they only mind when they are within hitting distance. J.D. stared at me and didn't move.

"Mom's calling you," he said to Grace.

"I know. Hey, come here," she said.

I could hear them but I felt as if I were in a room with one-way glass, like the psychiatrists often use to monitor children. I could see them and hear them but they would not respond. Just like everything around me. Like the personals and the war and the men. I can see them and I can hear them, but no one anywhere will respond. If only I could be Rosalind of Ganymede and run away to a forest and sing come-hither songs. If I could but be a fairy queen I would quick change all these irritants into suds in the sink and make all my dirty clothes into funny people who chatted and loved me. I would make every dirty spoon that falls behind the couch into a suitor; every marble that J.D. never plays with on his floor into a friend. All the empty diet Coke cans would be wolves outside the windows, and we would have to be clever to get rid of them.

"Grace!" I shouted again. This time, she turned and climbed down the black hill. "Didn't I say never to climb on that? You . . . you . . ." I was stuttering. "You could fall through the top and . . . sink down all the way till nobody knew where you were . . . and you'd . . . *die*!" I said.

Not long ago, some convicts broke out of a prison and were on the loose. J.D. and Grace and I were sitting in McDonald's having hamburgers for dinner when it was announced on the television. There is a TV in McDonald's that hangs over everyone's heads . . . suspended from the ceiling. It crossed my mind that it was a shame there was a TV in McDonald's. It was announced that six *desperate* killer men had dug their way out of prison and were headed this way. Well, it didn't say they were headed this way, but because of my upbringing I assumed they were. The children were cheerfully eating burgers and fighting over the fries . . . Shelley was spending the night at a friend's house . . . Only I knew the gravity of the situation.

"Excuse me . . . what did he say?" I asked an elderly man next to us in a plastic orange seat. "Huh?" he answered. "The man on TV said there were some convicts escaped . . ."

"I can't hear you," the man said. So there we sat, doomed.

It was particularly cold that night, the temperatures swooping down to zero. Hester wasn't home when I called, but later when I called her again she knew nothing of the convicts. "It said they had escaped on TV . . ." I said, urgency in my voice. "But I don't know if they were in Vermont or New York State . . . did you hear?"

"We've been at the hospital all afternoon. Then I was getting supper so I wasn't paying any attention." Hester called out to her husband if he knew where the convicts were escaped from, but he had fallen asleep in his chair in the living room. "That's what he does all the time now," Hester complained. "Sleep, sleep, sleep . . . I can't even get him to eat." I said I had to hang up. Darkness had slipped around our little pink house. The woodstove licked up the logs as fast as it could . . . I brought in enough wood for two days . . . in case we were unable to get out the door for some reason at least we wouldn't freeze to death. J.D. knew I was worried. "Will the six killers come here?" he wanted to know. He has such a sweet doughy trusting face. He has looked like he was made out of bread dough all his life. I named him after the country and western singer Jimmy Dickens. The last thing his father said to me as he was leaving the hospital where I was in mild labor was, "Name him after me, Gabby. It's a tradition in my family that the first born son be named Jefferson Dutton Pantaloni." At that point, we knew J.D. was a boy because I'd had an ultrasound.

"Never!" I managed to whisper. They had me tied to three different machines all monitoring different things . . . and I was being pumped full of this awful drug called ritodrine, which sounds like Dexedrine but is actually more like adrenaline . . . it makes your heart race, but it gets you out of premature labor. Jeff was dressed in his nicest trench coat and carrying a leather all inclusive briefcase with him as he dashed out the hospital doors for the last time. He wanted my son to be named after him . . . and I had only that one scud to retaliate with . . . *"No!"* I said, triumphant. And he was gone, because his parents had really disapproved of the match . . . and he was a Pantaloni and the Pantaloni family sticks together and doesn't cross the parents, which is rather sweet . . . rather romantic, except if you were in my shoes, then it was a tragedy. But in order for the family to agree to pay the hospital bill for my son (it was forty thousand dollars due to his premature birth), I had to name him what they demanded. So on his birth certificate it said J. D. FULBRITEN and they thought that meant Jefferson Dutton, but it doesn't, it means Jimmy Dickens.

J.D. offered to sleep in the same room as me that

night of the escapees . . . Grace too wanted to stay with me. I lay awake with my heart pounding like I was back on ritodrine, thinking how perfect my place was for six desperadoes. I began to imagine scenarios where they stole into the kitchen covered with mud from the tunnel they had crawled through . . . I would have to hide the children under a bed. I would take an iron pot from the pantry . . . No . . . How could I get to the pantry if they were already in the kitchen? Okay . . . they are on the porch about to come in . . . I hide the children under the bed and rush downstairs and grab a pan from the pantry . . . I meet them at the door and *slam*! One killer stands stunned, staring at nothing before he doubles over in pain . . . the other five cut off my arms and legs. The six killers have made their way into my bedroom . . . it is pitch dark and I wake up to the sound of them laughing. They are muddy from the escape and angry because they were on death row without having had a fair shake . . . they are desperate and nothing will stand in their way. I can't figure out how to save the children before getting killed myself.

The six convicts have arrived at my door. They tell me as they cover my mouth and force their way into the kitchen, "We are all from Cuba and have been convicted unfairly. None of us did a damn thing wrong except try to live in this country . . . you must hide us! In exchange, we will do any carpentry work that needs to be done around the old homestead . . ."

All night long I lay shivering in my bed. The wind made the old willow tree creak and clunk and at one point the cat terrified all of us when it jumped up on the piano . . . Grace cried because she thought one of the convicts was playing . . . In the morning there was no report in any of the papers about six escaped men who had dug their way to freedom . . . In fact, not a single person I talked to knew anything about it at all.

That did it. I sent the children off to school and sat down to compose a letter to Iggy. It was short and to the point. I said I had prayed and received an answer . . . if he would have me at this late date . . . I would be for time and all eternity . . . Mrs. Iggy Stains.

Hester does not want to come over and put her log cabin together at my house. I can tell. She says when I go visit, "I've got to put that log cabin quilt together for Larry's wedding . . ." but when I say, "Do you want to come over and lay it out on my kitchen floor? I cleaned up this morning . . ." she covers her mouth with one hand and hurries to her sink . . . "Well, he's not feelin' too good. I better stay in case he needs me . . . we'll see . . . we'll see what tomorrow brings," she says. And that makes my heart sink. I know that there are not any more like Hester for me to know . . . she is the world that was before . . . the simple happy life of the pioneers, of the innocent forties, when the women made sweaters for the men to wear in the World War

II trenches . . . she is the cheerful world of the one-room schoolhouses and "putting up your winter's food." There is no replacing her. When she is gone, that world, to me, is gone. What makes it hard is knowing she *isn't* gone, but the threat of her husband's illness has changed her. She turns on the TV and will not answer me when I say I hung some suet in my tree.

"Well . . ." I say, getting up and going to the door, "I guess I better go stoke my fires. If you want to do that quilt . . ." my voice falters a little.

"I'll let you know . . ." she answers, but her eyes are on *Guiding Light* on her kitchen black and white.

While I was at Hester's, the mailwoman has come and gone. And lo, she left me a letter from Utah.

MR. AND MRS. STAINS ANNOUNCE THE MARRIAGE OF THEIR SON IGGY TO SANDY SNOWS OF PROVO. R.S.V.P.

Gabby, I'd invite 'cha, but as you know because you do not hold a temple recommend you can't enter into the Salt Lake City temple for our marriage . . . Sandy and I are getting sealed for time and all eternity! Hope you find your place with heavenly Father someday too!

Iggy

Well, there goes my option.

Summer is approaching. Out by the old dump one can tell because Mr. Boots has returned with a new shipment of calves and assorted heifers, bulls that have been fixed and the like. He didn't wave as he went past the house and down into the lower fields, his truck full of swaying black and white hips and long swishing tails and feet shifting in the newness of the ride. I was in my yard, having a yard sale (America's once-favorite pastime—now a rather passé sport) and I saw him rattle past with the cows. He didn't even look at what I had out when he buzzed past with an empty truck later on. I had slaved to make this yard sale a success, but it was on the same weekend as a bake sale in town and a church social gathering and, sad to say, I was embarrassed of my own junk. I had velvet chairs and some old brass lamps and picture frames and lots of Steve Martin movies and a few stained kids' clothes . . . it's so horrible when you drag all your stuff outside to sell to someone else and it looks even shabbier outside than it did in your own house. And everyone looks at you like, "How could you ever own this stuff? What kind of homemaker *are* you? No wonder your husband left you . . ." Well, they don't say any of those things, but it's in the air. Lemme tell you, it's in the air.

"How much is this?" someone asks, holding up an antique box full of jet. Jet is black beaded stuff the Victorian ladies used to put on everything, especially when there was a funeral going on . . . or maybe they used it at their weddings. They used to wear black at weddings.

"That?" I say, suddenly shy, "well, ten dollars?"

The person drops the box like it is poison and walks away, fingering this and that briefly before getting in his car and roaring off. There may not be another car for hours out here. I pick up the jet-filled old jewelry box. "Too much. I should have said five dollars," I say to myself, but I think in my heart the person didn't know what it was and wouldn't have paid more than a quarter.

Letting things go feels very nice. Everyone in America got the hang of it a few years ago and yard sales have been rampant ever since. But suddenly, maybe the recession did it, yard sales have fallen by the wayside. After my yard sale did so poorly, I went to a few along the highway in town, and there were tables piled high with creepy stuff, horrible, desperate people standing glaring at you, holding a little cash box (probably empty), and sad children with their Barbies laid out in the sun tagged 50 cents. Women were selling their sewing machines, their mothers' kitchen tables; men were letting go the garden tractor, the rowing machine, tools, and their record collections. Everywhere there were beds set up with $40 stuck to their railings . . . or $5 takes it. And only myself wandering around a sea of junk, looking blankly at the stuff, unable to become enthused anymore over YARD SALE! YARD SALE! It is like Slicker lipstick and geodesic domes: a thing of the past.

So Mr. Boots is back. And so are his problems. Grace had been feeding the baby cows across the road for a whole afternoon. She was pushing clover mixture through the fence, she told me.

"Clover and some chewy grass and some dandelions. A nice mixture. Mommy, don't you love baby cows?"

So I had taken some notice of them. A day later, Mr. Boots pulled up at my continuing—and still pathetic—yard sale. He got out and walked toward the iron bed, then kept walking—past the broken chest of drawers, beyond the L'il Tike broken car and Happy Pumper gas tank and on into my backyard. His eyes were on the point above the trees. I thought he'd gone crazy.

"Mr. Boots!" I called out. "Something you're looking for in particular? I have a lot more on the porch . . ." but he said nothing.

I followed him out as far as my scallion patch and watched him disappear over the bank. That's where my land slides dangerously into ledges and cliffs and then the creek below . . . well, it's a river but they call it a creek in Leadbelly. I always think of it as a river. Maybe I'm wrong, though. Frankly, I don't know the difference between creek and river and brook.

I considered phoning the police. He had crossed my land with a faraway look in his eye . . . he might not be all that happy . . . perhaps farming has taken its toll on him. Maybe he lost a loved one in the brief Persian Gulf War. But then he reappeared and looked at my house and at me in the scallion bed. "Mr Boots?" I ventured.

"Cows are gone," he said. He looked at my house with what I thought was an accusing glance.

"Oh, my God," I said. "The babies? Gone? And no sign of blood or anything? I mean, I mean . . ." I was about to tell him we have a wolf out here, but I refrained.

"Thought they mighta gone out this way . . ." he said, sounding like he thought I had stuffed them in a shed on my land.

"Maybe they went that way," I suggested, and pointed toward the lower pastures.

"Nope. Can't . . . got that fenced off. The older ones are mean to 'em, so we have to separate 'em."

"Oh, I see," I said. "Well, they aren't around here I don't think," I said, feeling a little hurt. How could Mr. Boots think I had them on *my* land? I mean, I would never take his cows. Did he feel I was an unfriendly, unmarried woman? Is it the fact that I am unmarried that these people think I am some sort of danger? A threat to society? A menace to their herd?

"I'll call you if I see them," I said, and turned back

to my yard sale. Two kids were looking over the grubby stuffed animal collection.

"How much is this one?" a kid called.

"A dollar," I called back.

"Gee, I wish I had a dollar," the kid said, and turned to his friend. "Do you have any money?"

"Yeah, I've got lots!" the friend said, and pulled out some change. "Ten, twenty . . . fifty-seven cents. No, sixty cents." They were about twelve years old. New kids from the sad condos over the hill.

"Special on today only," I said, coming up to them. "Two bears for fifty cents." Then I gave them each one and they exchanged them for some cleaner ones and rushed off to tell their friends.

Mr. Boots stomped off down the road.

I'm going to write a letter to Iggy. I'm going to spill my guts . . . rather than let some intruder come and spill them for me, I might as well succumb to the idea of average marital bliss . . . though amorous is not how I would describe my feeling toward him . . . I'll at least write and congratulate him on his fine match to Miss Snows. Actually, the picture he sent is pretty . . . she looks a lot like the girl in the background. I wonder if that is her sister . . . Iggy and I never had a *heavy* relationship. We never *did* anything if you know what I mean. But, now that he is getting married or has already gotten married, the threat of it all has diminished and I feel, if not amorous, at least fascinated. *Fascinated* has married a lot of couples.

Of course, I'd never mail it but I could write and tell Iggy how I've always wanted to be his wife . . . "though I know polygamy is a commandment of the past," I could say, "I hope someday it will be reintroduced." I think there are too many single women out there who need a husband and plenty of married men who would like another wife. Supposedly it began when a lot of the men were killed off and there were widowed women all over the place . . . they called them "widowed sisters" . . . "So," I will say in my letter, "if it comes around again, please consider me for Mrs. Iggy Stains Number 2." Because really, I am not against being a "companion wife" as the Mormons used to call them.

Polygamy Pot Luck ######################

When there are more women than men at your gathering, consider this backup recipe to make a festive occasion for all.

1. ***1 or more men***
2. ***Belief that we all are able to live amongst each other as brethren***
3. ***2 or more women, fat, thin, pretty, not so, etc.***
4. ***Any other righteous additions***

Before heating oven, wipe slate clean. To each addition add kindly acceptance in abundance. Shake sense in. Remove any floating scum such as jealousy and heat to a roiling boil. Not a dish for everyone, but certainly everyone gets a dish.

Hours after he'd left, Mr. Boots returned, walking down the road in front of my house, with the four calves in front of him, shuffling here and there, wandering from side to side. Mr. Boots had a pail with him.

"You found them!" I called out from my porch. "Where were they?"

"Down't the grain store," he yelled back. "They went all the way down there for some grain . . . so I bought them some grain." He urged them now and then to keep moving in an orderly fashion toward their pasture. I went back inside—and noticed several hours later that Mr. Boots was still in the field with them, just standing around with his pail of grain.

Life Juice ¤¤¤¤¤¤¤¤¤¤¤¤¤¤¤¤¤¤¤¤¤¤¤¤¤¤¤¤¤¤¤

1. Women and men and children

2. A planet

3. Terrible sadness, great joy, dash of unrealism

4. Pinch of sex

5. 1 cup hope

Whip batter on high speed because this will heighten all desires. Cook over low flame because important things take time. Remove, when done, from heat and cool because nothing remains hot forever. End result will be a thin cloudy liquid. You should not be able to see through it. If you can, add more hope and repeat process. Pour into Thor's endless horn and drink. And drink. And drink.

God Bless